"How can you be mad as hell at me one minute and look like you want me to kiss you the next?"

Her head jerked back. "What makes you think—?"

The question ended in a shudder when he palmed her jaw, dragged his thumb across her lower lip. "You want a minute to think about your answer?"

"Yes," she whispered, closing her eyes as their lips met. But she was pretty sure a grin flashed across his mouth an instant before touchdown, even though she was equally sure—if not more so—that he hadn't said all that simply to manipulate the moment. Not Kevin, who was—

His free hand cradled the back of her head as his mouth—warm, firm, insistent—moved over hers before shifting to place little kisses at the corners of her lips, her cheeks, *that* spot behind her ear.

—completely guileless.

Incredibly good at this, but guileless.

Stupid, Julianne thought, in sync with his heartbeat, so strong and sure underneath her hand. *Wrong. Pointless. Crazy.*

Dear Reader,

From the moment our first son was born, my husband was a hands-on Daddy, big-time. Eagerly taking on changing, walking and rocking-to-sleep duties, he was the perfect blend of nurturing and protective. Now that our oldest is nearly thirty (while our youngest is a new teenager), we've long since realized that parenthood really is forever. Even when kids mess up. Or maybe especially when they do.

Kevin in *Baby, I'm Yours* was one of those kids who make parents jump every time the phone rings...and who make them extraordinarily proud (and relieved) when they finally get themselves straightened out. But it's not until he meets his baby daughter for the first time that he really, truly understands that a good father will do anything to keep his children happy and safe—that when they hurt, he hurts, too. And that there's no expiration date on a father's love.

Just ask my husband.

Karen Templeton

BABY, I'M YOURS

KAREN TEMPLETON

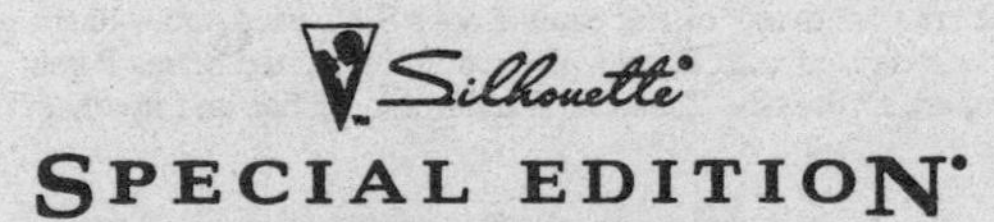

Published by Silhouette Books
America's Publisher of Contemporary Romance

ISBN-13: 978-0-373-24893-3
ISBN-10: 0-373-24893-8

BABY, I'M YOURS

This edition published by arrangement with Harlequin Books S.A.

Visit Silhouette Books at www.eHarlequin.com

Printed in U.S.A.

Books by Karen Templeton

Silhouette Special Edition

Marriage, Interrupted #1721
††*Baby Steps* #1798
††*The Prodigal Valentine* #1808
††*Pride and Pregnancy* #1821
‡*Dear Santa* #1864
‡*Yours, Mine...or Ours* #1876
‡*Baby, I'm Yours* #1893

Silhouette Romantic Suspense

Anything for His Children #978
Anything for Her Marriage #1006
Everything but a Husband #1050
Runaway Bridesmaid #1066
†*Plain-Jane Princess* #1096
†*Honky-Tonk Cinderella* #1120
What a Man's Gotta Do #1195
***Saving Dr. Ryan* #1207
Fathers and Other Strangers #1244
Staking His Claim #1267
***Everybody's Hero* #1328
***Swept Away* #1357
***A Husband's Watch* #1407

Silhouette Yours Truly

**Wedding Daze*
**Wedding Belle*
**Wedding? Impossible!*

††Babies, Inc.
†How To Marry a Monarch
**The Men of Mayes County
*Weddings, Inc.
‡Guys and Daughters

KAREN TEMPLETON

A Waldenbooks bestselling author and RITA® Award nominee, Karen Templeton is the mother of five sons and living proof that romance and dirty diapers are not mutually exclusive terms. An easterner transplanted to Albuquerque, New Mexico, she spends far too much time trying to coax her garden to yield roses and produce something resembling a lawn, all the while fantasizing about a weekend alone with her husband. Or at least an uninterrupted conversation.

She loves to hear from readers, who may reach her by writing c/o Silhouette Books, 233 Broadway, Suite 1001, New York, NY 10279, or online at www.karentempleton.com.

To Jack
who really is the World's Greatest Dad.
(And a pretty good husband, to boot.)

Chapter One

Kevin Vaccaro slouched behind the wheel of the rented compact, his left arm sizzling in the early-June sun. His stomach felt like that poor kid's must've on the last leg of his flight, right before the twerp hurled into the barf bag.

It's not too late to turn back.

He shifted out of the searing sun, watching the house. Ignoring the voice. On the surface, he was ready. He'd ditched the ragged jeans and baggy, wrinkled T-shirt he'd traveled in for a striped polo and khakis he'd borrowed from one of his brothers. He was combed and shaved and generally as presentable as he was gonna get without help from those gay dudes on that makeover show.

Inside, however, was something else again.

The house sat there, inscrutable. Aloof. Two stories. Yellow stucco. Recently painted white trim. A Spanish Territorial jewel, sparkling against a sky so bright it hurt to look at it, one gem among many in Albuquerque's casually upscale Country Club area near the river. Kevin had only seen it once before, when Robyn had taken him by to see where she'd grown up. It had been Halloween; they'd sat across the street for more than an hour, watching her father open the door over and over to dozens of trick-or-treaters—mostly kids minivanned in from other, poorer neighborhoods, she'd said—handing out full-size Butterfingers and Snickers and Twix instead of those wussy bite-size things.

He remembered the almost wistful envy in her voice. Weird, he'd thought at the time, through the haze of assorted controlled substances. Still weird, he thought, now stone-cold sober.

Whether Victor Booth was there now, he had no idea. The man wasn't exactly listed in the phone book. In fact, despite his regular appearances on one of the morning talk shows a few years back, even though you could hardly go into Costco and not see his face plastered on a stack of hardbacks, it was next to impossible to find out anything about "Dr. Vic." Apparently the paparazzi had bigger, blonder, boozier fish to fry.

A breeze nudged aside the heat clinging to Kevin's skin, rustled the cottonwood leaves, shimmering coins in the clear midmorning light. He sucked in a breath. Then another. Two thousand miles was a long way to come to possibly run into a dead end. But he had to find Robyn, to apologize for running, even if at the time he'd felt he had no choice. Then maybe he could finally get on with something resembling a real life. How he was supposed to go about that…not a clue. But for sure his Peter Pan days were over.

A grinning golden retriever edged into his peripheral vision, a toned matron in a sleeveless shirt and cargo shorts marching smartly behind. The woman glanced at the parked car, curiosity buzzing from behind bumble-bee-eye sunglasses. A second later, she flipped open her cell phone, tossing another furtive glance over her shoulder as she soldiered on. On a weary sigh, Kevin unfolded himself from the car, giving the woman—clearly keeping an eye on him—a little wave and smile.

She jumped, nearly tripping over the dog as she scurried away.

Feeling moderately cheered, Kevin hauled in another steadying breath and started across the street, thinking it was a shame Hertz didn't provide barf bags as part of the rental fee.

"What on earth are you watching so hard, Julie-bird?"

Ignoring her father's much-loathed pet name for her, Julianne McCabe shifted slightly at the living room window. All the better to see the tall, lanky male—the last vestiges of boyhood clinging to his loose-limbed gait—heading toward the house.

"See for yourself," she said, removing her glasses to clean the lenses on the hem of her sleeveless blouse. Pointlessly, as it happened, since her father, in his usual summer uniform of loose linen shirt and Dockers, had already hobbled across the room to peer over her shoulder. Smelling of aftershave and peppermints, like all good daddies should, Victor Booth was supposed to be in his office, working or resting the pulled muscle in his back or something. Not here, hovering. Being "there" for her.

Julianne pushed her glasses back on, wincing slightly when the corners of the steel frames caught in her too-long bangs. When had she last worn her contacts? Or makeup? Had the energy, or inclination, to fix herself up?

"Who the hell is that?" her father muttered a moment before the young man vanished behind the massive, obscenely blossomed Spanish broom blocking their view of the front entry. A second later, the doorbell rang.

And wasn't it a sad commentary on what she'd let her life become, that a stranger at the door should produce something almost like a thrill? Over the ripple of self-disgust, she said, "Guess we're about to find out."

"Don't bother. It's probably just somebody trying to either sell us something or save our souls."

Too late on that last thing, Julianne thought as she shook her head, aiming an indulgently patient look in her father's direction. The sort of look adoring and/or grateful daughters were supposed to give doting fathers. Especially fathers with the confidence-inspiring visage that sold books and filled auditoriums—the thick, tweedy hair and crinkly blue eyes, the precisely clipped hedgerow of also-tweedy whiskers edging a Dudley Do-Right jaw.

"Since he's empty-handed, I think we're safe," she said, heading toward the door, amazed to find herself almost awake. "And besides, he's been sitting in his car watching the house for ten minutes."

A cane shot out in front of her. "Stay here."

Julianne crept into the tiled entryway behind her father, who was shuffling toward the door as fast as his pulled back muscle would let him. Although what she hoped to see, she had no idea, since his Mack-truck build easily blocked the doorway. Gus, their older-than-dirt chocolate Lab, dozed on the warm, unevenly textured clay tiles in a blurred pool of sunlight from the clerestory over the doorway. *Wouldn't mind spending my days like that,* she thought, her arms folded over her stomach, only to realize she pretty much did. Except for—

"Sorry to intrude, Mr. Booth," said a strong New England accent. "My name's Kevin Vaccaro. I'm, uh, a friend of Robyn's? She here, by any chance?"

Julianne sucked in a breath over her father's, "No, she's not," his words riddled with grief, anger, regret—the same triad of emotions that had battered Julianne's soul, in never-ending waves, for far too long. Dad shifted to lean heavily on the three-pronged cane he'd already sworn to burn. "Robyn died three months ago, Mr. Vaccaro."

Blood drained from a face downright Michelangelo-worthy. No surprise there, given her sister's penchant for the cute but clueless, each hook-up less connected with reality than his predecessor, every one summarily dumped before they could dump her.

Except this one, who'd beaten her to the punch.

"I'm...so sorry," Kevin said, shock turning to horror in guileless brown eyes. "I didn't know.... I should go—"

"No," Julianne said, elbowing past her father, in a split second making a decision that would in all likelihood rock her universe. "No, come in—"

"Julie!"

"For heaven's sake, Dad, he's in shock! We can't just send him away!"

Confusion cramped Kevin's face as Julianne's presence seemed to finally register. Dimly, it occurred to her how she must look, the epitome of the haggard young widow who doesn't give a damn anymore.

"You know who I am," Kevin said.

"You bet your ass I know who you are," her father said. Not budging. Not forgiving. "And you are not welcome in my house."

"Dad. It wasn't his fault."

That much Julianne knew, even if her father still couldn't accept the truth: that Kevin's leaving Robyn, while not doing her any favors, had played little part in her inability to shake a substance-abuse problem that had been in place long before his involvement with her. Julianne also knew she'd win this battle. Although whether because Dad wasn't as adamant about his plan as he'd have her believe, or because he wouldn't deny her anything reasonably within his power to give her, she couldn't say. Nor did she care. At the moment she'd play whatever hand had been dealt her and deal with the consequences later.

"Can I get you something?" Julianne asked inanely, as she led Kevin past the quivering, gray-muzzled dog, the family photos lined up against a taupe wall—the Gallery of Illusions, Robyn had called it—into the brightly lit living room cluttered with corpulent leather furniture, local artwork, Southwestern native crafts. "Coffee? Water?"

"A beer?" her father said behind them, deliberately provoking.

Irritation flashed in toffee-colored eyes. Kevin was younger than she, she knew. Not by much, a few years. Enough to make a difference, though, to someone who felt old as Methuselah. His shirt was a little too loose, his pants rode a trifle too low, the hallmark of a guy who hadn't yet figured out that size mattered. Still, she thought—hoped?—she saw the signs of someone playing a hard, fast game of catch-up.

"I'm a recovering addict, Mr. Booth," Kevin said softly, reaching down to scratch a panting, grinning Gus between his ears before meeting her father's lockjawed expression. "I've been clean for more than a year." He turned to Julianne, wearing the slightly blank look of someone unsure of his next line. At the moment, the dog was probably registering more on his radar than she was. "And thanks," he said, "but I'm good."

Then he dropped onto the sofa's edge, his hands clasped between his knees as he stared at the floor, clearly trying to absorb the news. Finally he lifted his eyes to Julianne's father. "What happened?"

Victor's gaze bounced off Julianne's, scrupulously avoiding the baby monitor on the coffee table not two feet from where Kevin was sitting. Not that it was likely he'd make the connection, but still. "I don't have to—"

"I came here for answers," Kevin said, his voice surprisingly strong. Unintimidated. "No, actually I came to apologize to Robyn, but now that I'm here..." His hands clenched. "Now that I know..."

"This is private family business. We're not obligated to tell you—"

"My sister was killed in a swimming accident," Julianne said quietly. "While we were on vacation in Mexico."

Kevin swore, softly and bluntly, his reaction genuine enough for Julianne to feel a spurt of sympathy. Robyn hadn't loved him, she knew that much. Oh, she'd been pissed when he'd left, but that had been more the wounded pride of an emotionally scarred, and very young, woman outraged at being the dumpee. What Kevin's feelings had been for her sister, she had no way of knowing, of course. Not that she blamed him for leaving. Few people would have nominated her sister for a congeniality award.

Her father's eyes cut to hers, pleading. Unflinching, she returned his gaze, shaking her head.

Even though she knew what her act of defiance would cost her.

"Was she using?" Kevin asked, shattering Julianne's thoughts.

"Yes," she said over her father's "What concern is that of yours?"

"Of *course* it's his concern!" Julianne said, startled at her own vehemence. It had been a long time since she'd felt vehement. Since she'd felt much of anything. "It's always been his concern! He has a right to know! He's—"

"Julie!"

The cane jabbed into the carpet as her father advanced on her, his anguish colliding with hers. Her only excuse, perhaps, for not having fought him harder before this about ending the lie. But, oh, dear God—how incredibly out of whack their lives had been these past few months, focusing on loss instead of gain, on separation instead of connection. A crippling confederacy of negatives Julianne was now determined to overthrow—

"Don't do this, Julie-bird. Don't tell him."

—whether her father was on the same page or not.

"Don't tell me what, for God's sake?" Kevin was on his feet, his bewilderment clawing at her sense of decency. "Would someone please tell me what the *hell* is going on—"

Kevin's gaze jerked to the monitor, crackling with the distinct sounds of a baby waking up from her nap.

"Robyn was pregnant when you left," Julianne said quietly, her heart splitting in two as she watched her words slowly register in toffee-colored eyes.

When, all those months ago, good sense—and an awakening survival instinct—had finally shoved Kevin off the track to nowhere, he'd naively believed the temptation to backslide would never be an issue. At least, after those first few days. Weeks. Then it would get easier, right? Only he hadn't counted on fate lurking in the shadows, waiting for an opportunity to send him to his knees.

Because to be completely honest, he thought, as he gripped the rails of his baby daughter's crib, at that moment the sickly sweet promise of escape sounded pretty damn good. Except he knew there was no such thing as just one drink, just one toke, to dull the edge. Not for him. No more than he could take one step off a cliff and not end up smashed at the bottom. Literally.

The crazy thing was, he'd never really understood what had driven him off that cliff to begin with. His family was nuts, sure, but no worse than anybody else's. A lot better than most, actually. Why he'd hurt them, hurt himself, he had no idea. But even through the fog of shock, as his baby—oh, dear God: *his* baby!—fixed her calm, blue-gray gaze on his and smiled, pumping her chubby bare legs as she lay on her back, Kevin knew he would never, ever, do anything to hurt *her.*

Pippa, they called her. Short for Phillipa. Where Robyn had come up with that name, God only knew. Still, weirdly, it seemed to fit, he thought as he lowered one hand into the crib, his own smile far shakier than the baby's. Five chubby fingers curled around his index finger, snaring it in a death grip. Rosebud lips pursed, eyes went huge, chunky little legs ratcheted up the pumping to the next level. Despite Robyn's sister and father being right out in the hall, arguing—about him, no doubt—a soft chuckle broke the vise constricting his lungs.

He almost couldn't blame Robyn's father for not telling him. Hell, in his place Kevin wasn't sure he wouldn't've done the same thing, if somebody'd knocked up his daughter and then fled the scene of the crime. *But it wasn't like that, and you damn well know it,* a faint, barely comforting voice put in.

Yeah, well…

His finger still locked in his baby's hand, Kevin propped his other elbow on the crib rail to cradle his overstuffed head in his palm, as bitterness, disbelief and helplessness threatened to undo more than a year's worth of hard work.

Yet another tick-mark in the Kevin-screws-up-again column, he thought, heartsick. What the hell was he going to do? He barely felt confident enough to take care of himself, let alone anybody else. Yeah, he was beginning to think about settling down, focusing on the foreseeable future, but he wasn't there yet. At the moment he had no job, no home of his own and no funds, except for a small stash left over from what he'd earned helping his brother Rudy fix up his newly purchased inn in New Hampshire. How in the name of all that was holy was he supposed to take care of a *baby?*

Not that, if the heated discussion outside the door was any indication, Pippa's grandfather was about to let him.

Kevin shoved the heel of his hand into his forehead, trying to push out the dizziness. Talk about your one-two punches. First, Robyn's death, then—

"Are you all right?"

He hadn't heard Julianne come into the room. Or noticed when the arguing had stopped. Still, he definitely caught the slightly off-key note of judgment in her voice. Obviously, since she'd bucked her father about letting Kevin know about Pippa, she'd felt compelled to set the record straight. Didn't mean she was happy about it. Happy about him.

On a shuddering sigh, Kevin dropped his hand. "Not really, no," he said, his eyes still on his daughter.

"Sorry. Stupid question."

He almost smiled. "Where's your father?"

"Downstairs. Regrouping." She paused. "But don't get any ideas about grabbing the baby and making a run for it. He'd be all over you in a New York minute."

He shifted enough to catch Julianne's gaze, riveted to the baby. *And so would you,* he thought. But all he said was, "Yeah, I bet that cane could inflict some serious damage. Not to mention Killer, there."

Wagging his tail—after a fashion—the barrel-shaped dog hobbled over to lick Kevin's fingers, then collapsed at his feet with a sigh. Which Julianne echoed. "Okay, so Gus probably isn't much of a threat. But never underestimate a man who can still bench-press two hundred and fifty pounds. On his better days, at least."

"I take it he's pissed at you for going over his head?"

"He'll get over it," she said, unexpected steel underneath the softness. Another pause. "I know what you're thinking. But believe it or not, Dad's not a bad man. Just a hurting one. And I don't mean his back."

Kevin let the words settle into his brain, one at a time, before he said, "Believe me, you have *no* idea what I'm thinking."

"No," she said after a moment. "I don't suppose I do." Outside, a couple of doves hoo-hooed, off-sync. "She's a miracle, you know."

Kevin finally tore his attention away from the baby to really look at her aunt, still by the door. Sticklike arms pretzled across a white, shapeless top, over a pair of those pants that looked like brown paper bags with legs. Behind steel-rimmed glasses, pale blue eyes regarded him warily from deeply shadowed sockets. Cripes, the woman was so fair you could practically see straight through her, her shoulder-length hair as blond and fine as a little girl's. Even at her most wasted, Robyn hadn't looked that bad.

A few brain cells wondered what her story was, even as he said, "A miracle, how?"

"If Robyn hadn't broken her ankle in a fall right after you left, Dad might not have known she was pregnant until it was too late to intervene." Her gaze never left Kevin's, a bird keeping a steady, watchful eye on the thing that might eat her. "We basically strong-armed her into rehab, then refused to let her out of our sight for the rest of the pregnancy. If we hadn't..."

Another sour pang of frustration erupted in the center of his chest. "The baby's okay, then?"

"So far, so good," she said, her gaze shifting back to the baby. "She was a couple weeks early, but a good seven and a half pounds at birth. And she seems to be developing a little ahead of the curve. So we're hopeful."

Hopeful, but not sure. Now panic wiped out the frustration, that maybe she'd need special help down the road, and what if he didn't know what to do? Or couldn't afford it—?

"Dad was only following Robyn's lead, by the way," Julianne said. "About not telling you. She was convinced you'd abandoned her."

Kevin gnawed the inside of his cheek. "Since I didn't exactly leave a forwarding address, she wasn't that far off the mark. Even so, I wouldn't've left if I'd known she was pregnant. Even at my worst, I was never a total scumbag."

"Did you love her?"

He rubbed the baby's tummy, stalling. "Nobody was talking in terms of forever, if that's what you mean. Even if either of us had been capable of thinking more than five minutes ahead. Not something I'm proud of, but I'm not gonna lie about it, either. And Robyn swore she was on the pill."

"And you believed her?"

One corner of his mouth ticked up. "I hedged my bets, okay? But there was one night—"

"It doesn't matter," Julianne said quickly. "But in any case, it would have been difficult for Robyn to tell you since she didn't know herself. At least, I'm assuming her shock was real when the doctor delivered the news. What can I say? Logic was never my sister's strong suit. However, that's all water under the bridge. The only thing that matters now is the baby. Specifically, if you w-want her."

Kevin felt like he'd been sucker punched. Not because of her question, but because he couldn't immediately shoot back the "right" answer. Instead he sucked in a deep breath and said, "Wanting her isn't the issue."

"Of course it is. You either want to be a father or you don't."

Blood rushed to his face. "For the love of God, I just found out about this! I'm no more prepared now to be somebody's father than I was when the condom broke! Granted, my brain's less pickled than it was then, but I'd still figured on having more than five minutes before I had to start thinking about school districts and college funds. Maybe you have no clue what it feels like to have your life completely turned upside down, but right now I feel like rats are runnin' loose in my brain. So how about backing off and giving me a second to absorb a few things, okay?"

His heart thumping so hard his chest hurt, Kevin twisted around, his gaze dipping back to the baby, who was looking at him with wide, slightly worried eyes. *Way to go, bozo. Nothin' like scaring the pants off a five-month-old.*

A moment later Julianne crossed the room to clamp bony, blunt-nailed hands around the crib railing. A thin, diamond-studded platinum band loosely circled her left ring finger.

"Sorry," she breathed out, not looking at him. "I guess I'm still in a bit of shock, too. That you showed up out of the blue. I—we...just...want what's best for her. That's all."

Kevin looked at her profile, incredulous. "And you think I *don't?*"

"Sorry," she said again, tears in her voice. Brother. Was he batting a thousand today or what?

"Yeah," he breathed out. "Me, too. For yellin' at ya. Especially considering if it wasn't for you, I wouldn't even know about her." A pause. "Have you been taking care of her all along?"

Julianne reached into the crib, stroking the baby's cheek. "Yes," she whispered at Pippa's bright smile in response. "From the moment she was born." She angled her head at him, her lips slightly curved. "You can pick her up, if you like." When Kevin hesitated, she added, "Just make sure to support her head—"

"Yeah, yeah, I know." He sucked in a breath, then slipped his hands underneath Pippa's back and head, scooping the surprisingly solid little girl out of the crib to nestle against his chest. A whole mess of emotions slammed through him as she skootched around, her peach-fuzz head tickling his chin. But definitely topping the list was a gut-wrenching sensation of connection, that she was his, and he was hers, and nothing could alter that simple fact.

"You've done this before," Julianne said.

"I'm the youngest of six. Lots of nieces and nephews." Kevin shifted Pippa so her diapered tush rested in the crook of his arm. She started to fuss. Nothing major, just a few little eh-eh-ehs. Kevin gently jiggled her in his arms and she stopped.

"Is your family close?"

There it was, that same wistfulness he'd hear in Robyn's voice in those rare, unguarded moments when she slipped on her rebellious streak. "Closer than some of us might like," Kevin said, his lips twitching. "My three oldest brothers and their families all live within a cuppla blocks of my parents."

"And where is that?"

"Springfield, Mass."

"Ah. That accounts for the accent, I suppose."

"What accent?" he said, and she almost smiled.

"And your other siblings?"

She was avoiding the issue. The "what comes next?" part of the conversation. And thank God for that.

"My sister Mia's about to marry one of those hedge-fund dudes in Connecticut, over the July Fourth weekend. And my next oldest brother, Rudy, and his wife, Violet, just started runnin' an inn in New Hampshire."

Then there's me, he thought. *The caboose running his ass off to catch up.*

"Are they all happy?" Julianne asked.

"Sure, I guess. In an *Everybody Loves Raymond* kinda way. We yell, we fight, we screw up. Obviously," he said, with a self-deprecating half shrug. "Some of us've put our folks through the ringer more'n others. And my dad was a cop. It musta killed him sometimes, watching us learn things the hard way. But we're there for each other. Can't ask for more than that, I s'pose."

She watched him for a moment, expressionless, before walking over to dump out a laundry basket, full of tiny-footed sleepers and those one-piece undershirt things that snapped at the crotch, on top of the changing table.

"So what about you?" he asked, feeling the baby slump against his collarbone, drifting back to sleep. When Julianne glanced over at him, her brow pinched, he added, "What's your story?"

"My…story?"

"Yeah. You've been here for, what? A year, at least. But you're wearing a wedding ring. Does your husband live here, too?"

She pulled out a sleeper, quickly folded it. "Robyn never talked about me, then?"

"Not much, no."

"I'm a widow," she said quietly, not looking at him as she continued folding. Embarrassment cringed in the pit of Kevin's stomach.

"Oh. Hello. I'm sorry." Shrugging, Julianne opened the

drawer to a plastic bin on the changing table's second shelf, sticking in clothes as she folded them. "Was he sick? Unless you don't wanna talk about it—"

"My husband was killed by a drunk driver, Kevin," she said, the words oddly stripped of emotion. Kevin closed his eyes, bile surging in his throat.

"I'm sorry," he said again, lamely.

"Yeah. Me, too." Now bitterness trickled in to fill the void. "Gil and I had gone out to dinner. To celebrate my getting pregnant. It was pouring rain. Per usual for Seattle in the fall. We never even saw the oncoming car." Finally she looked at him, dry eyes screaming with unhealed grief. "So, actually, I know exactly what it's like to have my life turned upside down."

A silent, but potent, four-letter word exploded in his brain. "I can't believe Robyn didn't tell me."

"Clearly the two of you didn't have that kind of relationship," Julianne said, shoving more folded clothes into a second drawer. "And anyway, she and I weren't close. She...she wouldn't let anybody *get* close."

"You got that right," Kevin muttered, even as he caught the frustration, the disappointment in her voice. "But you didn't come out here right after, then?"

"Dad wanted me to. Well, after I got out of the hospital. There was a month of hell," she said dryly. "But I was determined to pick up the pieces of my life where I'd last seen them. It wasn't working, but I was being too stubborn to admit it. Then Dad discovered Robyn was pregnant, and it was obvious he'd never manage with her by himself, and I thought, okay, a diversion. Something to take my mind off...things."

Inside Kevin's brain, two and two slammed together hard enough to make his ears ring. "Even though..."

"Yes, even though I'd just lost my own baby a few months

before. But Dad needed me. Robyn needed me. And God knows, later on, Pippa needed me. What can I tell you? It felt good." She paused. "It still does."

Pippa was down for the count. Kevin turned to lay her back in the crib, for the first time noticing the pale lavender walls, the border of carousel horses prancing underneath the ceiling. As if reading his mind, Julianne said, "Robyn decorated the room all by herself."

"So she—"

"Wanted the baby? I'm not sure she knew what she wanted, to tell you the truth. She liked the idea of having a little girl to dress up. Being a mother, though…not so much." Julianne hesitated. "Dad and I have no idea where she got the stuff. In Mexico, I mean. Or when. But—" her lips flattened "—but there's a reason why Dad didn't want to tell you about Pippa."

"He can't possibly blame me for Robyn's habit."

"No, but you didn't exactly help things, did you?"

"I tried, Julianne," he said, hating, even as he weirdly understood, how he'd ended up the logical target for Julianne's and Victor's frustration and grief. "Believe me, I tried. But you gotta understand, every time I suggested maybe she go into rehab or get counseling or something, she went ballistic on me. Like you said, she wouldn't let anybody get close. Including me. And I finally realized I was having enough trouble keeping my own head above water at that point. So I ran. Except…" He streaked a hand through his hair. "The longer I was straight, the more I kept feeling like…I don't know. That I gave up on her too easily or something. Like maybe I *shoulda* pushed harder for her to get help."

"Even though you didn't love her?"

"Just because I wasn't *in* love with your sister didn't mean I didn't care about her, for cryin' out loud. When I started to get my act together, I really did want to help her go straight, too.

Only she wasn't gonna go without a fight, and I just didn't have enough fight in me for both of us. Not then."

Her steady gaze felt like it was gonna prick his skull. "The success rate for addicts—"

"Is, like, twenty percent, I know. Believe me, you can't throw a statistic at me I haven't heard a thousand times already. But what can I tell ya? You're lookin' at one of those twenty percent, okay?"

Her face colored. An improvement, frankly, over the ghost look. "Dad will still fight you for custody."

"Yeah, like that's a news flash. Well, here's another one—I may have made a crapload of mistakes in my life, but walking out on my own kid ain't gonna be one of them. No matter what I've gotta do to prove myself worthy of being part of her life."

After another long glance at his daughter, Kevin pulled out his wallet, extracting a plain white business card with his name and cell number. "I need some time to think, to figure out what the next step is. But I'll be back. And tell your father to not even think about taking my daughter away so I can't find her."

Julianne's mouth fell open. "He wouldn't do that!"

"Yeah, well, he already tried to keep us apart, so let's just say I'm not exactly feelin' the love here." He handed her the card. "You can reach me at that number. Anytime, day or night. And you can tell your father..." He hauled in a quick breath. "The pain I saw in his eyes, when he told me about Robyn? Why would he think I'd feel any different about Pippa?"

Then he walked away before the pain in Julianne's could fully register.

Chapter Two

"It's the best solution, Dad. And you know it."

From across the tempered-glass table on the flagstone patio, Julianne's father shot her an irritated look. "For whom?"

"All of us," she said, slipping Gus a piece of deli ham from her salad. Wide-eyed and very awake in one of her many baby seats, a just-fed Pippa babbled at the bouncing shadows cast by the thousand-fingered wisteria strangling the redwood trellis overhead. From the nearby pool, a chlorine-scented breeze danced around them like an attention-seeking child, as though trying to wick away at least part of the morning's turmoil. Fat chance of that.

"Bull," her father said. "And stop feeding the dog."

Her father had insisted on making lunch, despite it taking him three times longer than usual. Stubborn old fart. "It was one bite. And I'm eating. See?" Julianne shoved a forkful of red leaf lettuce into her mouth. It tasted, as everything had in the last eighteen months, like paper. Limp, oily paper. Blech.

"You haven't touched your bread, either," he said. "And it's the good stuff, from the bakery. With the chewy crust."

Julianne stared at the thick slice of bread her father had laboriously cut for her, fast morphing into a slab of concrete in the humidity-starved air. The bread stared back, baleful and unwanted. "I'm not that hungry." She twiddled her fork amongst the leaves, feeling petulant and out of sorts. *More* out of sorts. The sort of out of sorts that makes people say things they shouldn't. "I'm also not five."

"And you also don't weigh much more than you did when you were five. So, eat, dammit, unless you want me to drag you to the doctor."

Fine. So maybe she'd gone down a size—or two—since Gil's death. But if she wasn't hungry, she wasn't hungry. And anyway, what was the point of eating when you just ended up dead, anyway?

Okay, even for her that was probably a tad too morose.

And her father had changed the subject. She speared another chunk of ham. At her knees, Gus—definitely not in danger of starving anytime soon—whined softly and licked his chops, hopeful. The ham suspended in midair, Julianne regarded the top of her father's head, feeling, as usual, lost in the jungle of emotions being around him provoked. More often than not, though, once she'd machete'd her way through the frustration of living with the spokesperson for implacability, how could she not feel profound compassion for a man who'd never wanted anything more than for his children to be happy? That he'd been powerless to make that happen for either of his daughters…

Well. The least she could do was let the man make her lunch.

"It's just as well that Kevin found out now and not later," she finally said, steeling herself against the sting. "It would have only been worse for us—and Pippa—if he had. And now that he knows, he's not going to go away. Or forget about his own daughter. And the sooner you accept that the easier it's going to be."

Her father's fork clattered to his plate as his gaze slammed into hers. "And *damned* if I'm going to let some junkie take my granddaughter!"

At his sharp tone, Pippa began to whimper. Gus—who took his role as mother's helper very seriously—thoroughly licked the baby's blobby little feet, distracting her.

"He's not a junkie, Dad," Julianne said softly, helplessly smiling at her niece's recently discovered belly laugh. "At least, not anymore. And anyway," she added, returning her gaze to her father, "even Robyn said his major problem was alcohol, not drugs."

"That's supposed to make me feel better?"

"No, of course not. But if he's been clean for a year—"

"We only have his word on that, you know."

Julianne shakily set down her own fork, her half-eaten salad jeering her as she folded her arms across her stomach. She looked out over her father's lawn and much-prized garden, scrupulously avoiding the pottery studio he'd had built for her shortly after her arrival. *Screw water conservation,* screamed the lush, bright green, weed-free grass, the dozens of rosebushes in copious bloom, the masses of deep purple clematis and azaleas and rhododendrons camouflaging the eight-foot-tall privacy fence. Dad spent hours out here during the long spring and summer, coaxing humidity-loving plants to grow in a high-desert climate. The same love-doesn't-give-up mind-set, Julianne mused, that had made him the darling of the self-help circuit.

If you care enough, you can make it work, make it happen, make it bloom.

She returned her gaze to her father, thinking, *It must be hell, living a lie.*

Pippa started fussing again; Julianne slid out of her chair to heft the baby into her arms, Gus hovering to make sure she didn't drop her. As she inhaled Pip's sweet, baby-shampoo smell, she remembered Kevin's awestruck expression when he held his daughter for the first time…the fierce look in his eyes when, after the initial shock wore off, he realized he was going to have a fight on his hands. That second look, especially, had pierced straight through the vast dead space inside her, rudely jolting her out of her nice, safe, bland cocoon.

Bastard.

"I know a year isn't very long in the scheme of things," Julianne said. "That Kevin could backslide. But he is Pippa's father, Dad. He has the right to know his child. Which I've said all along."

That merited far too many seconds of her father's trenchant gaze. "You're projecting," he said gently.

"Because I lost my own baby, I'm empathizing with how he'd feel if he lost his? You betcha. But trust me, Kevin's not going to simply take off with her."

"You can't be that naive."

"I'm not. But you weren't in the room with him. I was. And I promise you, that man is no more ready to be a full-time dad right now than Gus." At the sound of his name, the dog waddled back to nuzzle aside Pippa's thigh, laying his head on Julianne's lap. She gave him another piece of ham, ignoring her father's glare.

He stabbed at his salad, winced, then shoved the bite into his mouth. "Then why on earth would you want to encourage him to *be* ready?"

"Would you rather he show up with a court order and just take her away?"

Her father's brows crashed together. "But you just said—"

"I didn't say he didn't *want* to be Pip's father. I said he wasn't *ready.* Once the dust settles, however, I have no doubt he'll change his tune. And if he does press the issue, I can't see where he wouldn't be within his rights. Pip is his daughter, after all."

"According to Robyn."

"So we'll do a DNA test. I doubt Kevin will object. But what did Robyn have to gain by telling us Kevin was Pippa's father? Especially since she didn't want him to know." Julianne fiddled with her lettuce some more, then lifted her eyes to her father's. "Be truthful—are you really up to a custody battle? Because I'm sure as hell not."

"So we should just hand Pippa over without a fight?"

"I don't want to lose her any more than you do. It's the fighting part I'd just as soon avoid."

Victor carefully leaned back in his padded chair; Gus the Fickle hobbled over to him, his long tail whapping Julianne's bare knee. "What do we even know about this kid? Aside from his dragging your sister down into the pit with him, I mean. Is he working? Does he even have any way of taking care of Pip?"

Julianne pulled the baby closer as she worked to bring her breathing under control. It wasn't that she didn't understand where her father was coming from. Or why. Losing Robyn—first to drugs, then to death—had nearly wrecked him. And God knew how Julianne would have gotten through the last year and a half without his support. But while her dad might have been the go-to expert on mending other people's family rifts, he could be spectacularly obtuse when it came to mending—or even acknowledging—his own.

"I'll grant you, maybe his earlier behavior wasn't the most mature in the world," she said at last. "And maybe we don't know what he's really like now, or if he's really changed. Or even if he *is* able to take care of a child. Even so, he didn't have to come all the way out here, just to check up on Robyn. So I'm willing to give him the benefit of the doubt, even if you're not."

She leaned forward. "But you have *got* to stop using Kevin as a scapegoat for what happened to Robyn. He said he tried every way he could think of to get her into rehab, but she refused.

And yes, I believe him," she said before her father could argue with her. "After all, she didn't exactly go meekly for us, did she? And we weren't trying to get our own heads straight at the same time. There was only so much he could do, Dad. Even you have to see that."

A bruised shadow passed over her father's features, followed by a sigh. Of acceptance? Resignation? Julianne had no idea.

"You always were the soft-hearted one, Julie-bird."

"Because I don't have it in me to keep a father and child apart? Then, yeah. Guilty as charged. In any case, the more obstacles we throw up between Kevin and Pippa, the worse it's going to be for all of us. But if we let Kevin stay with us..." She shrugged. "It's a win-win situation."

"And how do you figure that?"

"Because if he's here, we can keep an eye on him. Get to know him while he gets to know his daughter. But at the same time, maybe..."

"What?"

She turned Pippa around; pudgy, shapeless feet dug into her thighs as the baby pushed herself upright, Julianne's hands firm on her waist. The baby had recently discovered the wonder of noses. Now, with a drooly squeal, she batted at Julianne's, the little girl's innocent joy jostling loose—even if only for a few precious moments—the solid, putrid ache of loss. "Maybe," Julianne said softly, locking eyes with her niece, "if we *don't* fight him, he'll realize she's better off with us, after all."

Her father's sharp silence finally brought her eyes to his. He slowly pushed himself to his feet, angrily grabbing for the cane. "I've already lost two people I didn't fight for hard enough," he said, leaning so hard on the cane Julianne worried he'd topple over. "Damned if I'm going to let the same thing happen to my granddaughter. Maybe I can't stop Kevin from seeing Pip. But live in my *house?* No damn way."

As her father lurched off, grumbling, the dog slogging beside him, Julianne found herself sorely tempted to chuck the slab of rock-hard bread at his head.

Blinking until his eyes adjusted to the dim light, Kevin stood inside Felix Padilla's upholstery shop, thinking, *Welcome to my brain.*

Crammed into the narrow space like corralled sheep awaiting shearing, Victorian love seats in threadbare velvets mingled with Americana wing chairs, sets of Danish modern dining chairs with faded burnt-orange seats, camel-back sofas in worn brocades. Damn place looked like a 3-D encyclopedia of Ill-Advised Decorating Styles of the Twentieth Century. Just like it had the first time he'd seen it, more than a year ago. He followed the barely three-foot-wide walkway to Felix's workshop in back, where the jumble disintegrated into flat-out chaos.

"Felix!" Kevin called out, his pupils cringing again at the stark daylight lurking outside the open loading-dock door. Mind-numbing eighties rock blared from a dusty boombox on one corner of the massive cutting table; tools, swatch books, industrial sewing machines, bins of welting and studs and upholstery nails littered what little space wasn't taken up by a dozen sofas and chairs in various stages of resurrection. This was seriously the lair of a madman. A half-deaf, insanely talented madman who hadn't been without work since 1965.

"Felix!"

"Over here! Behin' the settee!" A bald, caramel-colored head popped up over the love seat, upended like a dead animal in an advanced stage of rigor mortis. "So," Felix shouted over the music. "You were gone a long time. What'd you find out? An' don't sit on that chair, it's jus' finished. The las' thing I need is a dirty butt print on it."

Kevin pointlessly turned down the radio: half-deaf men didn't know how to whisper. He'd met Felix through AA; he'd never forget the pride shining in the old guy's black eyes that night when he stood and announced—loud enough for God to hear—that he'd been sober for "seven t'ousand, two hundred an' thirty-six days." A week later, in a huge act of faith, he'd taken Kevin on as an apprentice, until they both realized heavier-duty intervention was called for. It was Felix who knew somebody who knew somebody else who got Kevin into the facility in Denver where the tide finally turned for good.

There were other people in Albuquerque Kevin could've hit up for a place to crash for a few days, but Felix was the only person he could trust. Who'd understand what he was going through.

The short, barrel-chested guy now cussing out his arthritic knees as he struggled to his feet had been uncle, confidant and rock-steady support to the messed-up hombre who'd finally swallowed his pride enough to admit he needed help. Felix had known all about Robyn. Had even suggested—sorrowfully, to be sure—that maybe Robyn was one of those people who'd have to hit rock bottom before she was ready to turn her life around.

Kevin leaned his backside against the cutting table, his palms braced on either side of his hips. After an hour of aimless driving around town, the double whammy had only begun to sink in, about Robyn, about Pippa. For the hundredth time, a white-hot jolt of adrenaline shot through him.

He met Felix's eyes. "Robyn's dead."

The old man sucked in a breath. "*Muerta?* No! *Dios mio*—when?"

"Three months ago."

"What happened?"

"Swimming accident. Down in Puerto Vallarta." Kevin could tell by Felix's eye roll that he'd mangled the pronunciation. "According to her sister, she'd been clean for months, but—"

"Her sister?"

"An older sister. She's staying with their father." His throat worked. "To help take care of the baby."

"The baby? What baby?" Another sucked-in breath preceded, "You got a *kid?*"

Kevin had long since stopped being spooked by Felix's Olympicesque knack for jumping to conclusions. Actually it took some of the pressure off, not having to spell everything out. "A little girl. Nearly five months old." He screwed a palm into his eyelid, then let it drop. The sympathy in the dark eyes in front of him made his own burn.

"What're you gonna do?"

"I have absolutely no idea."

The old man dragged a worn ottoman from underneath the cutting table, commanding, "Sit!" before waddling over to an ancient fridge and pulling out two Cokes. "You, my frien'," he said, handing Kevin one of the cans, "need a plan."

Kevin took a pull of his soda, nodding as the carbonation exploded against the roof of his mouth. "What I need is a job. And transport of some kind, since I hadn't planned on keeping this rental for more than a few days. So I can hang around for a while until I figure out what comes next."

"You got it," Felix said, slapping Kevin's knee. "Orlando, my assistant, he suddenly had to go back down to Juarez to look after his sick momma, I got work coming outta my ears. An' I jus' bought a new truck. You can use the old one if you want. She looks like crap, but she still runs, an' that's what counts, right?"

"That would be great, thanks," Kevin said, relieved. Upholstery wasn't his first love—he much preferred working on houses to recovering sofas—but he was good at it. And work was work. As wheels were wheels. He smiled. "Funny, you don't look like an angel."

A row of very bright, very straight teeth glinted from underneath a brush-roller mustache. "Are you kiddin'? You're the one who'd be saving my ass. So maybe I see God's hand in this, no? An' you can stay with me an' Lupe as long as you like. No, no, no," he said, his head swinging as one hand shot up. "No arguments. Maybe our place is no five-star hotel, but it's free. An' the food is great, yes? As long as you don' mind dodging Frannie's little rug rats. Her husband's done a runner on her again, the bastard."

Kevin smiled, wondering how it was that the people with the least to give were so often the most generous. The Padillas lived in a tiny, three-bedroom adobe in the South Valley, which would have been fine if it'd just been the two of them. But invariably one or more of their grown kids—with their kids—were in residence, too. Not that Kevin had issues with sleeping on the futon in their living room, but he hadn't planned on staying more than a night or two.

Yeah, well, he hadn't planned on discovering he was a father, either.

Another jolt. Damn, he was beginning to feel like a rat in a science experiment, getting a shock every time he went the wrong way in the maze.

And didn't that pretty much sum up his life?

A glance around the jumbled shop confirmed that Felix's offer hadn't been out of pity. "Okay, I'm in. At least until Orlando gets back."

"Put it there, my frien'," Felix said, hand extended, teeth flashing. He chuckled. "Only please tell me you can start right away. My back is killin' me."

"Deal," Kevin said, thinking, *One problem down, only five million left to go.*

Several hours later, after helping Felix make several deliveries, Kevin begged off to go apartment hunting. Not that he didn't appreciate his friend's offer, but obviously Kevin was going to need a place of his own. And soon. Someplace he could take his daughter. As it was, prying Pippa away from Victor wasn't gonna be easy. Without a job and/or a home? Fuggedaboutit.

Even if settling in Albuquerque hadn't been part of his plan. Okay, *plan* might be stretching it—truth be told, Kevin hadn't really thought much past squaring things with Robyn. Even so, although he liked the Duke City well enough, he'd always thought of it as part of his drifting phase. In terms of *then,* not *now.* And having finally mended a fence or two with his family, he'd begun to seriously consider returning to Springfield, give in to his sisters-in-laws' blatant attempts at fixing him up with assorted friends, sisters, cousins. Finding peace right in his own backyard and all that.

He hadn't told his folks about the baby yet. Although, after forty years of parenthood—not to mention all the hell *he'd* put them through—he sincerely doubted this would even register on the "You did *what?*" scale.

Pippa would make their fourteenth grandchild. Not counting the three extras Rudy and Mia brought to the table by virtue of falling in love with people who already had kids. There were towns in New Mexico with smaller populations than the Vaccaro clan, Kevin thought with a slight smile…one that flattened as he slowed down in front of, then drove past, yet another sullen-looking apartment complex that offered month-to-month rentals.

Sure, there were knockout apartments in the city, with stunning landscaping and pools and the like, places he knew Victor Booth would approve of. Places Kevin didn't dare sign a lease for until he nailed down a steady job. Not to mention, he thought, idling at a stoplight, drumming his fingers on the steering wheel as hip-hop vibrated from the car radio, all the baby crap he'd have to buy. Cribs and changing tables and strollers and…things.

And then there was the whole day-care issue. Finding it, paying for it, worrying about it.

Although...he could take the baby back home, he supposed. His parents certainly had the room, and there'd be more baby stuff than he could shake a stick at, and day-care options, and family, and he could probably find work without too much trouble, doing construction or renovation or whatever. And it wasn't like anybody could say anything. He was the baby's father for godssake.

So why didn't this feel more like a solution? Why, instead of feeling another layer of worries peel away, did he suddenly feel like hurling?

The truck's wheels scraped the curb as Kevin swerved into a parking space alongside one of the many little parks dotting the city. The door shoved open, he stumbled out of the car, gulping for air as he staggered toward a pool of shade underneath a large ash tree close to the brightly colored playground. Long, thick grass soothed his palms, cushioned his backside when he dropped onto it, tucking his head between his knees for a moment until the nausea passed. A bunch of little kids, under the watchful eyes of their mothers chatting at a picnic table nearby, took turns zooming down a blue twisty slide, screaming, thrilled.

One of the mothers reminded him of Julianne. Slender, blond, with glasses. Shapeless clothes. But a lot more lively—and louder—the woman's unfettered laughter carrying across the park.

Kevin forked both hands through his hair, remembering the look in Julianne's eyes when he'd handed Pippa back to her. When she'd told him about losing her husband. Her baby.

Holy hell, he thought as the light dawned—it wasn't *Victor* who'd be the biggest obstacle between him and his little girl.

And the longer she stayed with Julianne...the harder removing Pip was going to be.

He dug out his cell phone, his heart slamming against his rib cage for several seconds before he finally flipped it open.

His father answered on the first ring.

Chapter Three

Almost every evening—once the sun was at a kinder tilt—Julianne plopped Pippa in her stroller and took her for a walk around the neighborhood. The excursions did both of them good, getting Pippa used to different sounds and sights and getting Julianne out of the house—out of herself—without having to deal with the tiresomeness of being sociable. Occasionally they'd pass a lone jogger or cycler, an older couple fast-walking their way back to youth, but for the most part it was just Julianne and the baby and the quiet. She loved the quiet.

When she didn't hate it, that is.

Because while the quiet brought peace, it also provided a far-too-fertile ground for memories. For reflection. For the nagging little voice asking her exactly how much, and for how long, she intended to let herself rot away. This evening, of course, the stroller shimmying over the bumpy sidewalk as they headed back to her father's house, Kevin Vaccaro had joined the ranks of Stuff to Worry About. As in, what *would* he do? Would he take the baby...? *When* would he take the baby...? Would Julianne ever see her again...? Was there any way to solve this without somebody getting hurt? That sort of thing.

Sunlight flashed off a windshield as they turned the corner. Julianne slipped her cheapo sunglasses back on over her regular glasses, pushed the stroller hood forward before Pippa's squawk of annoyance could rev up to a full-out wail and thought, *Nobody told you to tell him the truth, dimwit.*

A sigh scampered to catch up with the thought. Because, damn her goody-goody conscience, she could never have lived with herself if she'd deliberately ignored the chance to do what was right. Now all she could do was trust that Kevin Vaccaro would do what was right, as well—

The sunspot on that windshield gradually diminished, revealing who was standing beside the from-hunger pickup surrounding it.

Well, hell.

"How'd you know we weren't inside?" she called before her brain alerted her throat to close and her stomach to knot.

In worn jeans and a loose T-shirt, Kevin leaned against the truck's dented front fender, anklcs crossed, arms folded across his chest, watching their approach through a pair of badass sunglasses. Julianne reminded herself she'd never been a big fan of badass. "I passed you on the way," Kevin said, in a voice deeper, and far more resolute, than she remembered. "You didn't notice?"

Julianne shook her head, releasing the stomach-knotting signals. *Amazing, the difference a measly eight hours makes,* she thought, halting in front of him, vaguely noting that the jeans were a huge improvement over the khakis. Because somewhere between then and now, the scraps of leftover boy still clinging to him that morning had slunk off into the sunset, leaving this...this badass.

"What…" She swallowed, started over in a more normal voice. "What are you doing here?"

"I said I'd be back." He removed his sunglasses, briefly met her gaze, then crouched in front of the stroller, his smile for his daughter absolutely heartbreaking. "So I'm back," he said in a voice as silky smooth as baby powder, setting off a fine trembling throughout Julianne's entire body that she could have gladly done without, thankyouverymuch.

Oh, hell. He was making her nervous. Which, he supposed, was the whole point to gaining the upper hand. Except, dammit, it was like scaring a whippet.

She'd led him through the house, out onto the covered patio. Flowers everywhere. Kick-ass trees. Lots of grass. Not a cactus or yucca in sight. Fair-size pool. Largish shedlike building in a far corner, a workshop, maybe.

"Have you eaten?" she asked, unstrapping the baby from her stroller.

Kevin turned, his gaze glancing off a straight ponytail, straight back, straight, shapeless sundress. Which probably wouldn't be shapeless if she'd eat something. Fill it out a bit. Yes, he knew some women were naturally skinny, but somehow he didn't think that was the case here. And what was with the gracious-hostess routine?

"I did, actually. After the meeting."

"The meeting…? Oh." She turned. "The meeting. Gotcha."

He almost smiled. "Yeah," he said, eyeing his daughter, contentedly gnawing her fist in Julianne's arms. He'd needed the extra boost, even after talking to his parents. Up until two minutes ago, he'd planned on telling Julianne and Victor right up front what his intention was. Partly so they wouldn't have time to react, partly before he lost his nerve. Now, however, he was thinking maybe the balls-out approach might not be the best way to go. That maybe it wouldn't hurt to sell the idea, little by little. "I just go to meetings when the mood strikes. But the ones who make it usually keep it up for the rest of their lives. You mind if I hold her?"

After a momentary startled look, Julianne's mouth twisted, like she was annoyed with herself. "Not at all," she said, her sandals slapping against the flat stones as she crossed to him, did the transfer. Pippa never noticed, far more interested in her knuckles than who was holding her. Julianne stepped back, arms crossed. Keeping an eye on him. "Maybe you should sit."

"I'm not gonna drop her, for cryin' out loud."

"Still," she said, eyes round with worry behind her glasses. Kevin sat. "What goes on at the meetings?" she asked. Still standing.

"Didn't Robyn tell you?"

"We had her in a private clinic. And if it hadn't been for the mandatory family group sessions, we would have known next to nothing. And besides, as I said…my sister wasn't interested in sharing."

"*Sharing* is the key word, actually," Kevin said, turning the baby to face him. "People share their stories. Their personal hells." Man, was this a strong kid or what, her head not even wobbling on that little linebacker neck. What he could see of the neck for the chins, he thought, grinning. Petrified. Still gumming her fist, shiny with baby spit, Pip grinned back; Kevin's heart did a triple forward somersault. "And their triumphs," he said quietly. "Even the littlest ones count. When you're climbing up from rock bottom, every step back up is a biggie."

After a moment Julianne eased over to perch on the end of a chaise across from him, her arms still tucked against her ribs, knees pressed tightly together, eyes fastened on the baby. She almost seemed to be shrinking into herself, like she was trying to become invisible. Panting, the Lab plodded over to sit heavily on one hip at her knees. One slender hand reached out to stroke the space between his ears, and Kevin thought, *Screw working up to this.* But before he could open his mouth, she said, "You're taking her, aren't you?"

He couldn't meet her gaze. "Yeah."

"When?" she whispered.

"I promised this upholsterer friend of mine I'd help him out of a bind, so probably not for at least a week."

"A *week?* How can you possibly make arrangements to take care of a baby in a week? This morning you said—"

"I know what I said this morning," Kevin said, finally looking at her. "But since then I've talked to my folks. I can live with them indefinitely. They've got tons of room, Ma's agreed to take care of Pip while I look for work—"

"With them? In Massachusetts?"

"It's where my family is. Like I said, we're close. Pip'd have a million cousins to play with—"

"So, what are you saying? Quantity trumps quality? That because it's just the two of us, Dad and I don't count?"

Aw, man—those eyes were killers. "Of course I'm not sayin' that. But I'm Pip's father. She belongs with me. And I'm gonna be honest with you, I have a far better chance of makin' it work back home, where I've got connections and a place to live, than I ever would here."

"Living with your *parents?*"

"What's wrong with that? It's working for you, isn't it?"

Her face went bright red. A second later she bolted from her seat and back toward the house. Muttering an obscenity, Kevin took off after her, cupping the baby's head as he followed her through the French doors into the living room. "Julianne! I'm sorry, I didn't mean—"

She whirled around, as though realizing she'd left the baby with him. "You have no idea," she said, trembling, "what it's been like for us. For me. Dad and I were just piecing together the scraps, trying to make a real family for Pippa! What's so awful about that?"

"Nothing! But my finding out about Pippa changes everything. I mean, you had to know, when you told me, what would happen!"

"Julie?" her father said, hobbling into the room. Julianne flew to him, crumpling against his chest. Wrapping one arm around his daughter, Victor glared at Kevin over the top of her head. "What the hell's going on?"

"I've decided to take Pip back with me to Massachusetts, Mr. Booth," Kevin said quietly. "In about a week."

Victor's deep blue gaze lanced Kevin's. "Before we get DNA verification that she's really yours? Over my dead body."

Okay, so maybe he'd been wrong about the Julianne-being-his-biggest-obstacle thing. Not that Kevin was about to back down, but at least he now knew where to focus his fire. "So we'll do the spit test," he said, jiggling the baby when she began to whimper. "But as soon as we know—" he forced down the grapefruit at the base of his throat "—she's mine."

A still-shaky—and, Kevin was guessing, somewhat sheepish—Julianne extricated herself from her father's arms. "Are you all right?" Victor murmured, worried, one hand on her shoulder. She nodded, shoving tears off her cheeks, and nausea walloped Kevin all over again.

"It's Pippa's bedtime," she said, fixing Kevin with watery eyes, her expression a weird mix of sympathy, resignation and an anguish so deep Kevin's heart squeezed in response. "Besides, the tension's not good for her."

Since the baby had begun to cry for real, even Kevin had to concede that point. Especially since he figured things were only going to get more intense. Julianne wiped her palms down her dress, then held out her arms. "You can check on her before you leave. Promise."

Kevin handed Pip over, then watched them leave. "Do you even love her?" Victor asked behind him.

Startled, Kevin turned. "What?"

"Pippa. Is this about loving her, or just staking your claim?"

"Any reason it can't be both?"

"Julianne said you looked scared to death when you first saw her."

"Hell, I felt like I'd been knocked into next week with a wrecking ball. That doesn't mean I don't love her. Or don't you believe in love at first sight?"

"You're not going to rack up any points by being a smart-ass, Mr. Vaccaro."

"And if it'd been up to you, I would've never even found out about my daughter. Believe me, winning points with *you* is the last thing on my mind."

"I ran a background check on you, young man," Victor said, his gaze never leaving Kevin's. "Long before you showed up. So I know that in the past ten years, you haven't held down any job for longer than six months. That you haven't stayed in one *place* longer than six months. That you've had your license suspended twice for DUI and were busted once for possession."

"Then you knew exactly where to find me all along, didn't you?" When the older man didn't answer, Kevin let out a dry laugh. "Well. Look on the bright side—at least I never applied for the job of son-in-law."

Victor's mouth pulled even tighter. If that was possible. "I was only thinking of Pippa's welfare—"

"Because you think I'm scum. Got it. And to be fair, I can see where you're coming from. Sort of. But unless you hired a really crappy P.I., you also know I successfully completed a three-month rehab program and that my record's been spotless since. And the DUIs were years ago. Or doesn't any of that count?"

"I've already lost Pippa's mother," Victor said. "Damned if I'm going to lose Pippa, as well."

A splotch-faced Julianne inched back into the room, still

hugging herself, clinging to her composure with everything she had. Kevin wished like hell there was some way to keep her from being part of the collateral damage.

"You don't have to stay, Julie-bird. Kevin and I can handle this—"

"I'm fine. And anyway, this concerns me, too." Her eyes touched Kevin's. "Right?"

"Absolutely," Kevin said before her father could protest. Then he pushed out a breath. "Okay, maybe on paper I don't come across so good. And I know I've got this problem with shootin' off at the mouth and sounding like I don't take things as seriously as maybe I should. But I would think if anybody would recognize a defense mechanism, Mr. Booth, it would you be you."

Victor's brows lifted, and Kevin thought, *Gotcha.* "Yeah, I've read a couple of your books. My counselor in rehab was a big fan. Surprise, right? But it's like I told Julianne earlier—I'm not that idiot kid anymore. Haven't been for some time. Which means I *know* my present situation isn't exactly ideal. In fact, since I found out about Pip this morning? I've been pretty much a mess, trying to figure out how to make this work. But the only thing I knew, the only thing I still know, is that I'm not about to duck my responsibility." He hesitated. "Not like Robyn's mother did to her. To both of you," he directed to Julianne, who looked like she'd been clobbered over the head with a large stick.

A deathly quiet fell over the room. "Is that what Robyn told you?" Victor finally said. "That her mother killed herself to *duck her responsibility?*"

"I'm guessing that's how Robyn saw it," he said, realizing his mistake as it finally registered how much this family had been through. "Whatever the reasons, that had to be rough on a twelve-year-old. No wonder she was so messed up."

Of course, her father's obsessive determination to make up

for what Robyn had seen as her mother's betrayal had a lot to do with Robyn's behavior, too. Even Kevin could figure out that the harder Victor had tried to compensate, the more stubbornly she'd withdrawn. But that was a road probably best left unexplored, at least for now. "Look, all you know about me is what you see in those reports—"

"And what my daughter said about you."

"No offense, sir, but Robyn probably wasn't entirely objective when it came to me. We didn't exactly have an amicable breakup."

"He's right, Dad," Julianne said, and Kevin's eyes cut to her profile. "You know yourself Robyn's talent at shaping whatever she said to fit the moment." Then, to Kevin, "It's true, she never really did get over our mother's suicide—"

"Julie, this is none of his business—"

"Of course it is," she said with surprising strength. "Like it or not, Pippa's existence makes Kevin part of the family. And he deserves to know as much about Robyn as we can tell him. Especially if…if he's going to take her to the other side of the country."

Was the chick wack or what? It had to be killing her, to back him up like this. So why the hell was she doing it?

"Even on her good days," Julianne said, "Robyn wasn't known for her objectivity. After Mom died…" She sighed. "She was still a kid. And no matter how many times we told her that Mom had been sick, that her death had nothing to do with anything we did, it was obvious she never quite believed us. Of course, I don't suppose it helped that Mom had promised to take her out for a rare just-the-two-of-them shopping and lunch spree the next day."

Kevin groaned, even as he caught the sag of failure in Victor's shoulders. "Yeah," Julianne said, "it was pretty bad. How do you convince a child not to take something like that personally?"

And how did you take it? Kevin wondered, watching her.

"From then on," Julianne continued, "every slight, real or perceived, got blown completely out of proportion. And she *hated* being the one broken up with."

Gus nosed her hand. Smiling slightly, she gave him a pat, then looked back at Kevin, her brow pinched. "However valid your reasons for leaving her may have been, no matter how she really felt about you, all Robyn saw was that you'd screwed her over. That sent you straight to the top of her *S*-list," she said with a slight smile. "So you're absolutely right—she definitely wasn't a reliable source. Especially about you."

Not exactly a wholehearted endorsement, but better than a kick in the 'nads. "Mr. Booth," Kevin said after a moment, "it's not like I don't understand how this is hard for you. Especially since you *don't* know me worth squat. You also don't know my family, who were every bit as hurt by what I did as you were with Robyn. Believe me, if I go back there? If they thought I was even thinking about slipping back into old habits, *they'd* take the baby away from me. They're good people, Mr. Booth. They don't live in fancy houses or drive expensive cars, and all the kids go to public schools, but dammit..."

His eyes burned. "They *never* gave up on me. Even at my lowest point, I knew that. You know what my father used to say? 'When a kid comes in all muddy, you don't throw him away, you wash him off.' Somehow, I'm betting you'd agree with him."

After a very long moment the older man released a long, shaky breath. "Yes. I would." Then his jaw locked again. "But for all I know, you could be pulling a major con on me."

On a dry laugh, Kevin shook his head. "You know something? For somebody who preaches about forgiveness and healing as much as you do, you sure don't seem real good at practicing it."

Victor looked taken aback. But only for a moment.

"Ten thousand."

Kevin frowned. "Pardon?"

"Ten thousand dollars. If you agree to stay for a month. Providing you live here, in this house, so I can see for myself that you've changed."

"Dad!"

"It was your idea, Julie-bird," Victor said, and Kevin thought, *What the hell?* His eyes ping-ponged from Julianne back to Victor.

"Excuse me," he said when he could breathe again, "but I don't have to prove a damn thing to you. Not after the stunt you tried to pull on *me*—"

"*Twenty* thousand," Victor said, unfazed. Determined. "Deposited into your bank account at the end of the month to spend as you choose. If you agree to stay the month."

Incredulous, Kevin snorted a laugh. "And I cannot believe you're trying to buy my daughter."

"Oh, for heaven's sake—how stupid do you think I am? The only thing I'm trying to 'buy' is a month of your time. To make sure Pippa would be in good hands with you. You say you love that little girl, but I *know* we do. If you're determined to take her, then at least give us a chance to get used to the idea. To get to know you."

"Never mind that nobody gave *me* time to get used to the idea of being a father."

Victor's mouth tightened. "Touché. Still. We both know you're not in a position to turn down the money. Even today, twenty grand can go a long way when you have a child to take care of."

Kevin narrowed his eyes. He wasn't that stupid, either. Or that much of a fool. He knew damn well that Pippa would be more than taken care of, whether Kevin agreed to go along with Victor Booth's plan or not. He'd be very surprised if the trust fund wasn't already set up. Besides that, though, the old guy wasn't about to jeopardize his granddaughter's welfare to get back at Kevin. And after talking things over with his own father, he felt a lot more certain that while Victor might make noises about hauling Kevin's ass into court, his chances of gaining custody weren't all that great. Because the minute Victor brought up Kevin's past, he'd be asked how he knew. And the minute *that* came out, it'd be pretty clear he'd deliberately kept Pippa's existence a secret.

Sure, maybe Kevin's record wasn't exactly stellar, but he hadn't used for more than a year, he would be taking Pippa into a stable environment—at least, one stable enough for all reasonable purposes—and, oh, yeah, he was Pippa's father. He would submit to the DNA test to shut the old man up, but he wasn't worried about the outcome. God knows, Robyn may have had her issues, but Kevin and she had been virtually living together for the month before they broke up. He'd bet his life the baby was his.

However, he'd also be lying if he said twenty grand wouldn't come in handy. He could invest it, use it as a nest egg to maybe start his own renovation business. Sure, part of him wanted nothing to do with Victor Booth's money. But another part of him felt like, you know, the dude owed him. Pride was all well and good, but there was a fine line between pride and idiocy.

And at least, if he was in residence, nobody could play the "he hasn't been part of the child's life" card against him.

Kevin slid his hands into his front pockets, looking Victor straight in the eye.

"You swear that after a month, I can take her? No arguments, no threats?"

"You have my word."

"Oh, I'll need more than your word. I want this in writing, signed and notarized. About the money, too."

Victor's eyebrow raised, like he didn't expect Kevin to be that much on the ball. "Then…you won't mind if I add a paragraph stating that if you backslide, even once, we get her back?"

"Not at all. Because that's not gonna happen." Kevin extended his hand. After a moment Victor took it.

And Kevin prayed like hell that this time, he'd made the right decision.

Chapter Four

Trailed by Gus the Ever-Faithful, Julianne followed Kevin outside, as though she was in one of those dreams where her limbs seemed to have minds of their own. She only went as far as the end of the walk, however, watching helplessly as he continued walking to that pathetic excuse for a truck, only vaguely wondering—or caring—what had happened to the rental car. In the mauve light, an almost chilly breeze rustled the cottonwood leaves, released the broom's heady, spicy scent. "I swear I had no idea that was coming," she finally croaked out, hands fisted in her dress pockets.

He turned, smirking. "Even though it was originally your idea?"

So much for hoping he'd missed that part of the conversation. Dear God, if he had any idea what had motivated her initial suggestion… "Only your staying with us. The money thing was all Dad."

"And right now you're thinking, *Nice to know he can be bought.*"

Gus let out a soft, whiny woof. Frowning, Julianne glanced down the street at that woman who clearly used her poor golden retriever as cover for her snooping. Then she looked back at Kevin. "If he'd offered you twenty grand to leave Pip with us altogether," she said, knowing Ms. Snoop was too far away to hear, "would you have taken it?"

"*What?*" he squawked. "I wouldn't've left her behind for a hundred times that. Are you nuts?"

His indignation made her smile. "Then you're not a man who can be bought. Bargained with, maybe, but not bought."

The truck door groaned when Kevin swung it open. "No matter how you look at it, this is a crappy situation." His gaze, opaque in the dusky light, drifted to hers, "And nothing's gonna change in a month, which makes it even crappier."

"Why do you say that?" she said, propelling herself onto the sidewalk, a thousand thoughts jostling for position in her brain. Gus stayed behind, benignly observing the retriever. "Why couldn't you find work here? Permanent work, I mean. A place of your own. I know it's not ideal, but...between what you want and what Dad wants, maybe there's a compromise?"

A slight smile poked at the corners of his mouth. "Maybe there is. Like you said, I'm a man who can be bargained with. As long as there's no question about my daughter living with me, I don't suppose *where* I—we—live matters." Then the smile stretched. "But let me get this straight—you thought I should stay in the house, only then you changed your mind—"

"Actually, it was Dad who shot down the idea," Julianne said quickly, playing the conversational equivalent of three-cup shuffle. "So technically he changed *his* mind."

"Man," Kevin said, frowning slightly, clearly trying to figure out which cup hid the truth. "He really must be desperate. Considering that whole I'm-scum thing."

"It's not that bad," Julianne murmured, suddenly much warmer than the temperature warranted.

"Yeah, it is. But it's not like I can't relate. Your father and I might be on opposite sides here, but we both want what's best for that little girl. If his gut's churning over this half as much as mine is…I just get where he's coming from, that's all. What I can't figure out, though, is you."

Julianne flinched. "Me?"

"Yeah. First, why you took my side when you obviously don't want to give Pippa up any more than your father does. Second, why you looked like you'd just been hit over the head with a frying pan when your father came up with his little 'deal.'" His eyes turned into slits. "Call it a stretch, but I'm guessing you're not all that hot on the idea of me being around."

Not a stretch at all, she thought, then said, "What I want is neither here nor there. I defended you because somebody had to. Because Dad's grief over losing Robyn has made him completely myopic. He wants somebody, anybody, to be the bad guy here. And unfortunately you walked right into the line of fire. And Robyn…well. We already covered that ground."

She shivered. "Still. I may be willing to give you the benefit of the doubt, but that doesn't mean you're off the hook. Not by a long shot."

Irritatingly, one side of his mouth lifted. "Message received," he said, then finally slid behind the wheel, slammed his door, drove off. He was all the way to the end of the block before Julianne realized her knees were locked in place.

She unlocked them, went back inside. Her dad was in his office, at his computer. Probably working. He hated being interrupted. Ask her if she cared.

"Geez, Dad," she said, plopping into the armchair across from his desk. Gus collapsed at her feet, worn-out. "A little warning might have been nice. Twenty *grand?* Are you out of your *mind?*

Why on earth would Kevin be inclined to leave Pip with us now?"

Her father plucked off his glasses, then leaned heavily into in his high-backed leather chair, rubbing his eyes. When he looked at her again, she saw a weary resignation in those eyes that almost frightened her. "He's right, you know. As long as he's clean, I don't have a chance in hell of winning a custody battle. But there might be a slim chance that your idea *will* work, that he'll decide after a month she is better off with us."

So Kevin was right—her father *was* desperate. Grasping-at-straws desperate in a way she'd never seen him before, not even right after her mother died. With that, the fight drained out of her. "I wouldn't hold my breath on that."

"I'm not. But at least this way our butts are covered. A lot can happen in a month, Julie-bird."

Suddenly she got it. "You don't believe he'll stay straight, do you?"

"You know how many alcoholics actually stay on the wagon?"

"Yes, actually. But why do you automatically assume Kevin won't?" And why was she still defending him? "He already has a year under his belt. And that was without any outside motivation. Now, with Pippa…" Her eyes got itchy. "I'm just worried you're setting yourself up for a major disappointment, Dad."

The sharp ache of failure glittered in her father's eyes. "We thought we were home free with your sister, too. That even though we'd forced her into recovery, for her own child's sake she'd want to *stay* clean. And look how that turned out."

After a moment, Julianne propelled herself to her feet, dislodging the sixty-pound foot warmer. When she got to the door, however, she turned around, her brow knotted with the effort to focus her thoughts into words. "You know, it's not exactly in my best interest, either, if your theory about Kevin proves to be wrong. And yet I can't see myself sitting around, waiting—hoping—for Kevin to fall on his face just so you'll win, either. There's something about him..." She shook her head. "He's not Robyn, Dad."

Dad sighed. "He talks a good talk, honey, I'll give you that. But that's no reason to feel sorry for him."

"I don't feel *sorry* for him, dammit! I'm not even sure I like him all that much, to be honest. I just think he's a guy trying to fix his mistakes, who wants to be with his own child. He's not the bloody devil, for crying out loud!"

"Julie-bird—"

"And for the love of *God* will you stop calling me that? I'm not a freaking child!"

She waited a moment to absorb her father's stymied expression before leaving the room.

Kevin tossed his duffel onto a plaid club chair in Victor's guest room, next to a heavily draped window overlooking the backyard. The room was okay, if kinda impersonal. Inoffensive. Like what you'd find in a better-grade motel, maybe. But the bed—queen-size, with one of those fourteen-inch mattresses—was a damn sight better than Felix's futon. Place was a helluva lot quieter, too.

Speaking of whom... Felix definitely had a lot to say about this most recent development. Tact wasn't exactly the old guy's strong suit. Except, Kevin frankly wondered if his friend's loud objections weren't due more to his losing what he'd hoped was a buffer between him and Lupe than to Kevin's moving into Victor Booth's house.

Kevin unzipped his bag to load his few shirts, a couple pairs of jeans, into one of the cedar-scented bureau drawers. A clotheshorse, he was not. Wear it, wash it, repeat until replacing was the only option, was his motto. Somehow, he doubted the girl child snoozing peacefully next door was going to subscribe to the same fashion philosophy, if the piles of baby sleepers and what-have-you he'd seen Julianne folding earlier was any indication. Not to mention his nieces, all of whom could sniff out a mall from fifty miles away.

"Here."

Kevin turned to see Julianne standing in the doorway, bearing linens and ambivalence, a grinning Gus at her side. "Thanks," he said, crossing the springy Berber carpet to take them. The linens, anyway. Man, that conflict in her eyes *stung*. But whatever was going on underneath that pale blond hair—aside from the obvious, that his being there threatened her status quo as far as Pip was concerned—was off-limits. For the next month he was under her father's microscope, and he had no intention of letting anything, or anybody, distract him from the task at hand. Which at the moment was to make up his bed. He whisked off the tailored, earth-toned spread to reveal a thickly quilted mattress cover.

"Want help?"

He flicked a glance in her direction. Damn, she looked ready to keel over. "I meant it when I said I could do this myself."

"I'm sure you can," she said, stepping close enough to grab one corner of the fitted sheet when Kevin flapped it out over the mattress. Gus planted his butt on the floor, supervising. "But it goes much more quickly with two people. Besides, it's not as if I have anything else to do."

From a lot of women, Kevin might have taken her move as a thinly veiled come-on. Not this time. Far from it. In fact, she never once looked at him the entire time they made up the bed. Or even spoke. She might as well have been a robot, her movements quick and efficient, her face expressionless.

"How old's the dog, anyway?" he finally said, just to crack the silence.

"Gus?" The dog's ears perked up. "Twelve." Tossing a freshly cased pillow up by the headboard, she smiled affectionately at the beast, who took it as a signal to come get some love. "He was a pup when Dad brought him home for Robyn, a month or so after Mom died." Another pillow joined its companion. "She refused to have anything to do with him. Um...there's a bath across the hall," she said, obviously not up for discussing the subject any further. The bed done, she resumed her by-now-familiar crossed-arms stance. "Nobody else uses it, so feel free to spread out. And if you get hungry, it's open season on the kitchen." The corners of her mouth pulled up. "Dad always buys far more food than the two of us can possibly eat, so I'm always throwing half of it out, anyway."

Kevin could hear his mother's outraged gasp from clear on the other side of the continent. "Okay, thanks."

"Well. If there's nothing else...?"

Honestly, she was making him feel like he should tip her or something. "No, I'm good."

"Then...I guess I'll see you in the morning...."

"What about the baby?"

Her almost invisible eyebrows formed a vee behind her glasses. "What about her?"

"Is she sleeping through the night yet?"

"Oh. Not always, no. But—"

"I'm not here as a houseguest, Julianne, I'm here to take care of my daughter. So is there a bottle ready? Or do I need to fix it?"

As tired as she obviously was, Julianne still found enough oomph to glare at him. "I understand why you're here, Kevin. But maybe *I* don't need the aggravation of dealing with a freaked-out baby at 3:00 a.m. who has no idea who you are yet. I'll show you the ropes tomorrow, I promise. Until then, could you please just give us *all* a minute to adjust?"

He blew out a breath, then nodded. "Of course. I'm sorry. It's just...I don't want to give your father any cause to think I can't do this."

"Oh, trust me," she said, her exhaustion hanging over her like a cloud. "You'll have plenty of opportunity to prove yourself."

So he kept his promise when he heard Pippa bawling around midnight.

And again at two-thirty.

And somewhere around four.

When she went off at seven-thirty, however, he was there.

Aunts with martyr complexes be damned.

The baby's cries barely penetrated Julianne's quasicoma; she felt as though she was trying to swim through mud, knowing she had to claw her way to the surface but unable to fight the relentless suction pulling her back under. Finally, though, she broke through long enough to haul herself up onto one elbow on the daybed across from Pippa's crib.

A multilimbed blob that may or may not have been Kevin shimmered in and out of semifocus for several seconds, while the rest of her body slowly assimilated the assorted messages her sleep-deprived brain was sending out.

He glanced over his shoulder. She thought.

"You're awake," he said, his voice a rumble.

"That's a matter of opinion," she croaked, pushing herself to a sitting position and cramming on her glasses. And if she'd been a normal woman, if this had been a normal situation, if she'd had more than four hours total sleep the night before, the vision in front of her might have actually—she yawned—goosed the odd hormone or six. Instead, the sight of a bed-headed Kevin Vaccaro in boxers and a loose T-shirt barely registered a *Not bad.*

Somehow, Julianne thought as she halfheartedly mashed down her hair, she doubted she'd even rate that. After another moment or two to make sure her heart was pumping sufficiently to supply blood to extremities, she stood, then shuffled barefoot to the crib, her knee-length sleep tee fluttering around her thighs.

Kevin had already changed Pippa and dressed her in a lightweight sleeper with tiny roses all over it.

"Does she always wake up that much during the night?"

Julianne shook her head. Carefully. "No. At least once, always. Usually twice. I think she was showing off for you," she said, her heart expanding despite her exhaustion when the baby smiled for her. Kevin picked up the baby, already balancing her expertly in the crook of his arm, his broad hand firmly on her upper back and neck. Julianne got a whiff of warm, just-out-of-bed male and thought, *Whoa, Nelly.*

"So you sleep in here?"

She shrugged. "It's just easier."

"I take it your Dad's not helping out because of his injury?"

Even in her befogged state, she knew a leading question when she heard it. She was also too tired to lie. "He doesn't hear her," she said, the words sounding lame, even to her. "By the time I wake him up, I might as well just take care of her myself."

"So you've been basically getting no sleep since…since Robyn…"

Julianne unfolded her arms to mess with one of Pippa's constantly moving feet, Kevin's gaze hot on her face. "Robyn was a very sound sleeper, too."

Beats passed. Heat radiated. "Go back to bed," Kevin said softly, and she looked up at him, groggily thinking, *Don't be nice to me or I may have to hurt you.*

"She needs her bottle."

"Julianne, I slept in a room with my oldest brother's three-month-old twins when my sister-in-law broke her ankle and he was working the night shift. Believe me, I can figure out her bottle. How many ounces is she taking?"

She blinked at him two or three times before all of that finally registered. "A full bottle. Eight."

Kevin frowned. "How often?"

"I don't know. Every two to three hours? What?" she said when Kevin glowered at her.

"No wonder she's up half the night. The kid's probably *hungry*."

Julianne looked at Pippa, whose expression seemed to be oddly accusatory, then back at Kevin. "The doctor said she didn't need solids before six months."

"Yeah, well, ask my sisters-in-law how well that worked for them." He laughed. "Honey, this here's a Vaccaro. She was probably born craving lasagna. We need to get something substantial in that tummy, don't we, sweetheart?"

His gentle kidding with the baby only slightly mitigated the burst of anger that ignited inside Julianne's skull and quickly *whoomphed* over the rest of her.

"Well, excuse me, buster, but I've been taking care of this baby 24/7 practically since she was born. So how dare you waltz in here, doling out advice like you're God's gift to child rearing!" She tried to wrestle the baby from his arms, but it was like trying to pry gold out of a rock with a toothpick. Or a pair of toothpicks, in her case.

"Julianne," he said with irritating calm for a bed-headed man in boxers. "I'm not God's gift to anything. Trust me. And I didn't mean to step on your toes. I'm just suggestin' that it might not hurt to try a little rice cereal or somethin'. So how about we ask her doctor, okay? Okay?" he added when she didn't respond. Because she was too busy working on her grump face. When she finally nodded, he blew out a sigh. Then he said, "Now. You look like hell. And you sound worse. *Go back to bed.* Pip and I will be fine. And no, I promise I won't give her bacon and eggs."

Julianne might have smiled if she hadn't been so damn mad. And confused. And, yes, dishrag tired. In fact, right on cue, she yawned.

"But don't you have to go to work…?"

"It's Saturday."

Dear God, now she was losing track of what day it was.

With a nod, she started to leave, only to turn around again. "She goes down for her morning nap around ten, but she'll be up again in an hour—"

"Got it."

Then something occurred to her. "You won't—" She clamped shut her mouth, embarrassed.

"Abscond with her?" Kevin said. "Uh, no. Since spending twenty to life in prison for kidnapping isn't exactly part of my game plan."

"I'm sorry," she said, her face burning. "It's just…"

"I know," he said gently. "It's okay. Not get the hell out of here. And I don't want to see you downstairs before noon. Got it?"

She practically ran from the room.

Kevin was guessing it had been a while since the kitchen had been updated, if the mustard-gold cabinets and off-white appliances were anything to go by. Not that everything hadn't probably been top-of-the-line when it was new. Just that "new" had been a while ago. Then he noticed as, Pip firmly held in one arm, he started opening and shutting doors looking for baby-feeding paraphernalia, the telltale signs of a room about to undergo a metamorphosis: the experimental splotches of paint on one wall, three or four granite samples spread out across the worn laminate, a folder marked "Kitchen Re-Do" in bold, black magic marker.

"You're up early."

Kevin swerved toward the breakfast nook. Newspaper in one hand, cereal spoon in the other, Victor scowled in his direction. At his knees, Gus alternately licked his chops and politely whined.

"Thanks to Little Miss Alarm Clock here," Kevin said, shifting the baby slightly in his arms. "Although I'm usually up by now, anyway." Pippa had begun to gnaw on her fist; Kevin figured he had about thirty seconds before she realized it wasn't gonna do the trick. But when he went to put the baby into the high chair against a far wall, Victor said, "She's not ready for that yet."

Kevin recalled the wrestling match when he changed her diaper. Far as he could tell the kid was ready to start gymnastics training. Besides which the high chair was one of those numbers that adjusted, like, fifty different ways. However, since antagonizing her grandfather was not on Kevin's To Do list that morning, he instead asked, "You okay with holding her while I fix her bottle?"

"Of course I can hold the baby, I'm not crippled for God's sake. And the stuff's in that cupboard over the sink, before you go through every damn one."

Still gumming her fist, the baby settled happily enough on her grandfather's lap. Until she noticed his bowl of cereal. With a screech, she lunged for it. "Oh, no, you don't, Miss Fussy Pants—that's not for you."

The screech instantly ratcheted up to a howl. Kevin bit his lip at the face the baby made when Granddad tried sticking a definitely unwelcome finger in her mouth. Unfazed by the caterwauling, Victor asked, "Where's Julianne?"

"Hopefully asleep." Kevin checked the instructions on the can, filled the bottle with eight ounces of water, dumped in four scoops of formula. As he shook the bottle, he looked over at Victor, still trying to keep chubby little mitts out of his corn flakes. "I sent her back to bed. Pip woke up three times last night."

"You're kidding?"

"Nope." Kevin grabbed a clean dish towel before plucking his daughter out of Victor's arms and settling at the table with her. Pip latched on to the bottle like she hadn't seen food in weeks, chugging it down so fast he half worried she'd choke. "Geez, slow down, cutie, nobody's gonna take it from ya." He sat her up a little straighter on his lap, wiping a stray dribble of formula off her chin with the dish towel, then returned his gaze to Victor. Who was watching him like a hawk. Kevin glanced around. "Looks like you're thinking of a remodel in here."

"Thinking about it's about all I can do at the moment," Victor said, pulling a face a lot like the one his granddaughter had just made. "Damn doctor told me I didn't dare do anything strenuous for at least a month, unless I want to aggravate my back all over again."

"You were going to do the work *yourself?*"

"A good portion of it. The painting, of course. The floors." He tried to twist around, winced. "And I was thinking seriously of stripping and restaining the cabinets instead of installing new. They're solid maple. The baby-poop color had not been my idea, believe me."

"That's a lot of work."

"For an old man, you mean."

"For anybody. I just helped my brother refurbish a hundred-year-old inn. I'm still not sure how we got through it without killin' each other."

Victor's mouth twitched. "I've always done most of the work around here myself. Or with my father, when the place was still his." He gazed outside, Kevin supposed toward a bank of rosebushes reflecting the dappled, constantly shifting light from the sun glancing off the pool's surface. "For all these years," Julianne's father said, "through all the upheavals, this place has been the one constant. The one thing I could count on. Working on the house, the garden…" He looked over at Kevin. "I guess you could say that's *my* therapy."

Whoa. Totally not what he expected. Acutely aware of Victor's unrelenting scrutiny, Kevin set the half-empty bottle on the table, then propped the baby against his palm, rubbing her back until she let out a belch to do Homer Simpson proud. Then he settled her back into the crook of his arm to finish her breakfast. "Did we just have a civil conversation?"

"It's early yet," Victor said. "I'm off my game." When Kevin chuckled, Pippa's grandfather shoveled in a bite of cereal and said, with grudging approval, "You're not doing too badly."

"Hey. Anybody with two good arms who walks into one of my brothers' houses usually gets a baby shoved at 'em. You catch on quick. Speaking of which...what's up with Julianne's being the only one doing the night shift?"

Victor's eyes zinged to his. Kevin could practically see the hackles from where he sat. "I would if I could—"

"I'm talking about *before* you hurt your back."

"And I repeat, I would if I could. Or rather, if Julie'd let me. But she swore it wasn't necessary, that Pippa wasn't waking up all that often."

"Have you actually *looked* at your daughter recently? Or did it escape your notice she looks like something out of *The Night of the Living Dead?*"

"I look at Julie every damn day of my life!" Victor retorted. "And for your information, big shot, she looked a helluva lot worse a year ago."

"You're kidding."

"No, I'm not. So you can just stable the high horse." Shaking with emotion, Victor crumpled up his paper napkin and tossed it into the pond of soggy cereal in front of him. "I had no idea the baby was keeping her up at night, but that's because Julianne didn't tell me, not because I don't care or am too lazy to help out or think it's her 'job' to take care of the baby! Are we clear on that?"

Feeling like a primo idiot, Kevin lowered his eyes to the baby, sucking air out of a drained bottle. "That came out harsher than it should've," he mumbled as he propped Pip on his shoulder until she burped again. "But I've seen that new-baby-zombie look a time or six. So I was just wonderin' what was going on."

Victor slowly got up to stiffly carry his dishes to the

counter, grimacing when he tried to turn too quickly. "You know Julie's a widow?"

"Yeah. She told me." Kevin sat Pippa on his lap. She certainly wasn't ready to sit up on her own, but her little head was steady as a rock. He wiped up more dribble with a napkin; she smiled at him, batting her hands, and Kevin's heart turned over in his chest. "I'm guessing she's still pretty broken up about it?"

Victor's gaze clung to Kevin for a long moment before settling on his granddaughter. "Julie usually gives Pip a bath after her morning bottle—"

"I'll do it," Kevin said, grateful for the subject change. "Where's the towels and stuff?"

"Julie keeps a basket in the pantry with all her bath things. I'll run the water while you get it."

Baby clamped against his ribs, Kevin retrieved the wicker basket filled with towels, washcloths, baby shampoo, a pad to lay her on while he undressed her, a foam dealie to keep her from sliding around in the sink, some rubber bath toys. The minute Pip heard the water running into the sink, she began to squeal in anticipation, her feet thumping his stomach.

Kevin undressed her, then gently lowered her into the tepid water. A huge, gummy smile instantly bloomed as she smacked at the water, splattering her cheeks and eyelashes. She looked startled for a moment, then let out a huge belly laugh. And lunged for the rubber ducky Victor had dropped into the water with her. Silently thanking whichever ancestors were responsible for his big hands, Kevin held her firmly in his grip, even as he wondered how on earth Julianne—whose hands were half the size of his—managed.

"Julianne says wet clay might be slippery as hell," Victor said beside him, clearly not about to let Kevin bathe his granddaughter unsupervised, "but at least it doesn't wiggle."

"Clay?"

"She's a potter. Or was," he said, his words heavy as that wet clay. "But I don't think she's worked at all since Gil's death. Certainly not since she's been here, even though I built her a studio, a month or so after she came to help out with Robyn."

"The building in the corner of the garden?"

"That's right. Had utilities run out there and everything. The kiln alone cost more than my first car. To my knowledge, she's never even set foot in it."

Kevin cupped his hand to pour water over the baby's downy hair. Pippa gasped, then scrunched up her nose and giggled at him. "That's a lot of trouble to go to for a, um, temporary arrangement."

"How long she'd be here wasn't an issue," Victor said, a warning note in his voice. Which Kevin decided to heed. For the moment, anyway.

"Maybe she's just been too tired to work?"

"Could be. But somehow..." Julianne's father shook his head, then poked at the ducky bobbing in front of the baby. She immediately batted at it, spiked-lashed blue eyes going wide when it spun around.

"From the moment they're born," he said softly, "hell, even before that...you worry. You want to somehow protect them from ever getting hurt, even though you know that's not possible. The little stuff—the scraped knees, the ordinary disappointments—those aren't so bad. Oh, your heart aches right along with them, but you know they'll get over it. The big stuff, however..."

Kevin was just as glad he had to keep focused on the wet, squirming baby so he didn't have to look at Julianne's father. But that didn't do a damn thing to relieve the uncomfortable knot in his stomach, that he wasn't going to like where the conversation was headed.

"After the girls' mother died," Victor said, "I was at a complete loss. Not just for myself, but as a father. My training, my experience...suddenly, it all meant squat. Talk about something I couldn't fix."

In the silence that followed, Kevin said, "That...must be one of the hardest things a family can go through."

"It's that nagging voice," Victor said quietly, "that you could have, should have, done something to prevent it. That's the worst. Especially when Robyn—"

He sighed. "I did whatever I could—canceled my book tours, took a leave of absence from the TV show—but nothing seemed to work. In fact, the harder I tried to help, the more she seemed to resent me. As much as I blamed myself for her mother's death, Robyn blamed me more."

"Yeah, I kinda figured that," Kevin said. "That sucks."

Victor grunted, then nodded toward the sink. "The water's getting cool. Maybe you should take her out now?"

As it happened, Kevin had already reached for a hooded towel to drape over his chest. A second later he hauled Pip out of the bath, wrapping her up in the soft, warm towel, gently rubbing the hood over what there was of her hair. When she snuggled against him, looking for her thumb, Kevin felt a pang of connection so strong he had to shut his eyes for a second.

"Julie, though..." Letting the water out of the sink, Victor kept an eye on Kevin as he redressed her. "Maybe because she was older, or maybe because her nature's so different from Robyn's...she seemed determined to make things normal again. I've always thought of her like this duck," he said, shaking water off the toy before setting it in the drainer. "No matter how hard you push it underwater, it always bobs back to the surface, right side up. And I guess, the more Robyn seemed determined to destroy her life, the more I unconsciously relied on Julianne to be the stable one, the sane one. The one who'd always bounce back. I never worried about having to fix her, because she always somehow fixed herself. After Gil's death, though..."

His sigh seemed to fill the room. "It was as if she'd been punctured. She still floated to the surface—she still functioned, she even tried to resume her life in Seattle—but she couldn't find her way to right side up anymore."

Kevin leaned back against the counter, gently rocking the drowsy baby, torn between wanting the space to absorb all these new feelings about being a dad and getting sucked into everything Victor was saying about Julianne.

"You think maybe she worked so hard at being strong for you and her sister after her mother's death, there wasn't enough left to bounce back after losing her husband?"

"Exactly," Victor said, wearing a definite Listen-up-because-I'm-about-to-make-a-point face. "Which is why I hesitated asking Julie to help me when Robyn was pregnant. I wasn't sure she was up to it. Who knew she'd grab on to the idea like a lifeline. Helping me with Robyn, then Pip, apparently gave her back a sense of purpose that months of therapy couldn't even dent. The puncture is still far from healed. Obviously. And I know she overdoes it with the baby. But you have to understand—right now, Pippa's probably the only thing keeping her going."

After a long, tortured silence, Kevin said, "That your roundabout way of laying a guilt trip on me?"

"It's my way of letting you know how complicated this all is. Why I did what I did. Kevin…I lost one daughter because I wasn't really listening to what she needed. This time I'm determined to listen or die trying. To give Julianne *whatever* she needs in order to heal. And from the way you're holding Pippa, my hunch is that you already understand what I'm talking about."

He felt like he'd been shot in the heart with a nail gun. "Yeah. I get what you're talking about, all right. Mr. Booth…look, I feel terrible about everything that's happened to you and Julianne. Life's dumped on you both, but good. And it's not like I'd ever keep you and Pip from seeing each other. You're her family. But if you're asking me to sacrifice my daughter for yours—"

"I'm asking you—if the DNA test proves you're Pip's father—to think long and hard before you make a final decision."

Then Victor left, the dog waddling behind him. Sinking onto the nearest chair, Kevin rubbed his cheek over and over Pippa's peach-fuzz head, feeling like a fire was raging inside his chest.

Chapter Five

By Sunday evening, although Julianne was grateful her father had stopped moving like the Tin Man before Dorothy found his oil can, she wasn't nearly so sure how she felt about the way Pip was reaching out to Kevin as though she'd known him all her short life.

Ambivalence: the curse of being conscious.

When Kevin had ordered her back to bed the previous morning, she somehow doubted he'd meant her to stay until dinner. And then go back to bed at nine and sleep until ten. *The next morning.* Julianne might have been tempted to feel impossibly decadent, if she'd been awake enough to feel anything.

And now that she *was* awake—

"So how do you like your burgers?" Kevin said from the grill, muscles bunching and shifting and such when he rolled one shoulder to rub his face into his T-shirt sleeve.

—she was suddenly ravenous.

"As long as they're still recognizable as meat, I'm good," she said, thinking, *This will never do.*

"Got it," he said, not looking at her. "Victor, you?"

"Rare."

"Dad," she said, because she had to, "you know you're supposed to cook hamburger all the way through."

From over by the table, as he set out potato salad and toppings, her father grunted. "So tonight I'm living dangerously."

Feet up on a chaise, the baby propped on her lap, Julianne frowned. Who knew hell could be so pleasant?

Because let's recap, shall we? She was a thirty-year-old widow living with her father, with no discernible plans to change that scenario anytime soon. The father of the baby she loved with all her heart was not only living under her—okay, her father's—roof, but might very well take said baby to live on the freaking other side of the country. And the faux civility that had sprouted between Kevin and Dad while she was out cold was making her teeth hurt.

Yep. Definitely hell. And yet to the casual observer things might seem quite pleasant indeed: the charcoal-scented air was the perfect can't-feel-it temperature; it had been a good half hour since her father and Kevin had snarled at each other; she had an adorable baby girl on her lap and a first-class view of one of the finer male backsides she'd seen in some time. As long as she didn't think about either the past or the future—or why she was even noticing male backsides, fine or otherwise—she could almost believe she was...okay. Happy, no. But *okay* was a whole lot better than miserable.

God, she was sick of *miserable.*

"Here ya go," Kevin said, holding a plate in front of her on which lay a burger large enough to feed a family of four. Julianne shifted to set the baby in a seat beside the chaise, nearly doing herself a mischief as she bent over to strap her in. When she straightened, Kevin handed her the plate, immediately turning back to the grill to dish up his and her father's burgers, and some tiny, obviously insane part of her thought, *Look at me, dammit.* Because despite Kevin's earlier lack of inhibition about looking her in the eye, now he seemed determined not to.

And this was bugging her, why? Especially considering that, since Gil's death, catching any guy's eye hadn't exactly been a high priority, for one thing. And for another, if she remembered correctly Kevin's gaze was pretty…scary. And who needed scary in her life? Certainly not her.

But there it was, in all its glorious illogic.

"How come you're not eating?"

Julianne jerked at Kevin's voice, realizing she'd wandered so far down the path to Pointless Thoughts she'd forgotten about her food. "Sorry," she muttered, taking a bite. A rather large bite, actually. And then another, as Pippa squawked at her from below and Gus gave her sad, tiny, starving eyes from her other side. From the table, Kevin watched her, amused.

"I'm guessing it's okay?"

"Mmm," she said, nodding, sopping up dribbled hamburger and tomato juice with her napkin. "'Licious. Where's Dad?"

"He got a phone call. He went inside to take it." He watched her stuff an escaped bit of beef back into her mouth. "You must be feeling better."

Chewing, she shrugged. "Better? I suppose. The question is, will I ever feel *normal* again?"

Good God—had she actually said that out loud? To somebody she barely knew? Julianne stared for a moment at her mangled hamburger, half tempted to ask Kevin what he'd put in it.

After a moment of very telling stillness, she looked up to discover he'd apparently called a moratorium on the not-meeting-her-gaze thing. "What?"

Shaking his head, Kevin took another bite of his burger. "Forget it. I've already gotten my butt in enough slings around here by not knowing when to keep my big trap shut."

"So you'd rather let me speculate?"

He seemed to consider this for a moment. Then he nodded. "Yep."

"Then now's probably as good a time as any to tell you I have an incredibly active imagination."

Kevin set down his burger, took a long swallow from his tumbler of iced tea. "Okay," he said at last. "But not one word about how I'm sticking my nose in where it doesn't belong."

"Got it," she said uncertainly.

With a heavy sigh, Gus struggled to his feet and wandered into the yard. As Julianne watched him lumbering off, Kevin said, "I'm sure as hell no expert on any of this, okay?" and her eyes zinged back to his. "Not like your Dad. And God knows I haven't gone through anything near as awful as you have. But it seems to me, if you're defining 'normal' in terms of what you had before, then—this is just my opinion, okay?—that's probably not gonna happen. But…"

His forehead creased, he stared off into the distance for a second, then looked back at her. "It's just that you hear all these stories about how people recover from wars and floods and hurricanes and all kinds of crap, and it makes you realize how frickin' resilient the human race is, y'know? So I'm thinking you can probably do it, too. The only thing is…you gotta want it, Julianne. You gotta…I dunno. Believe you're worth it, I guess."

Breathing hard, she lowered her eyes to her plate, not sure whether the dizziness was due more to his being dead-on, or his being intuitive enough to *be* dead on. Speaking of resilient—clearly whatever he'd been doing all those years hadn't dimmed his thought processes one whit.

And, intuitive or not, he hadn't drawn his conclusions out of thin air.

"And here I thought you and Dad weren't really talking," she finally said.

"He talked. I listened. He's worried about you, Julianne." She heard the scrape of metal on flagstone as Kevin shifted his chair. "That you're healing too slowly. After what he went through with Robyn," he said, very gently, "I can't exactly blame him."

Her head snapped back up. "So sue me for not exactly being ready to sign up for some online dating service."

"Nobody's saying you should. But doncha think thirty's kinda young to fold up your tent? Not just about another relationship, about, well…everything. Now, see, you're pissed. Just like I said you were gonna be."

"I'm not pissed, I'm…okay, I'm pissed. Because for one thing, who the hell gets to decide how long is too long to grieve? And second, isn't it my decision what I do with my life?"

"Hey," Kevin said, pressing a hand to his chest. "I'm just offering my opinion. What you do with it is up to you."

"And when you had what Gil and I had—"

The clatter of Gus's metal feeding dish on the flagstone made her jump. They both looked over in time to see the dog clamp his teeth around the bowl's rim, then cart it over to the patio door, where he stood, wagging his tail. A second later the door slid open and Gus disappeared inside. Julianne took a deep breath, then said to Kevin, "I'm sorry, you're right. I have no business going nuts on you when I pushed you to say what was on your mind. But the thing is, I don't want another relationship."

Kevin's brows dipped. "Ever?"

"No. And not because I'm not 'over' Gil. But because I have thought about it. And getting involved with someone else…it wouldn't be fair to the other person. I'd always feel, well, like the next guy was a substitute for Gil."

"You're kidding. You honest-to-God believe that was it for you? That you don't get a second shot?"

Even though incredulity more than censure colored his words, Julianne still felt a fizz of annoyance at having to justify herself. "No, I don't. Maybe it works that way for some people, but not for me. It didn't for my father. There was someone, for a while, after Mom died, but..." She shook her head. "It never panned out."

"Wow," Kevin said. "Must be something, feelin' that strongly about somebody."

"You never have, I take it?"

His head wagged. "Nope. I've seen it, plenty, but I've never felt that kick to the gut personally." Then his eyes shifted to the baby. "I take that back," he said softly. "I had no idea I could fall so hard, so fast, for another human being." Chagrin tugged at his mouth. "All the junk I put into my body, lookin' for that elusive, perfect high... Who knew just looking at my own kid could give me a rush a hundred times stronger than some stupid chemical."

Amazed, and strangely touched, by Kevin's candor, Julianne could only stare at him as, right on cue, Pippa squawked again. Julianne looked down to see the baby's gaze latched on what was left of her hamburger. She had the feeling if the kid could get out of her baby seat, she'd be fighting her for it. "Mine," Julianne said. "*Now* what?" she said to Kevin's chuckle.

"Nothing."

Julianne chomped off another hunk of her burger. Chewed. Swallowed. "You think maybe we could put off hamburger until she at least has teeth?"

Grinning, Kevin polished off his own burger and got up to spring his daughter from her seat. "Betcha she'd be thrilled outta her Huggies with baby cereal, though," he said, launching into some dance routine—Julianne used the term loosely—that looked as though he was trying to stomp out a grass fire. Barefooted. This accompanied by some sort of hip-hop number he was apparently making up as he went along. He couldn't have looked, or sounded, more like a goofball. And he clearly couldn't have cared less, a realization that sent a slight tremor of envy through her.

That his heart was still intact. That he had the heady, delicious thrill of falling in love ahead of him. That at some point, if all went well, he'd feel for some woman what she'd felt for Gil. And she found herself saying a little prayer, that whoever she was would love him back, and that they'd have years and years and years to enjoy that love.

Ah. Now she knew what was in the hamburger: ground-up Hallmark cards.

Julianne shook her head, focusing again on the scene in front of her. Unable to choke back her laugh at Pippa's wide-eyed expression as she clearly tried to figure out what on *earth* the strange man was doing. Except then Kevin bounced three times in succession, and Pippa let out this squeal of glee, and Kevin smiled at her as though she'd given him the best present ever, and Julianne's heart turned over in her chest, at how natural he was with her. How good. Out of his gourd, but good.

Her eyes burned, remembering Gil's face, when she'd told him she was pregnant. How much he'd looked exactly like that, a mixture of amazement and tenderness and utter and profound happiness. Then Pippa apparently homed in on a speck of hamburger grease or something on Kevin's T-shirt, bunched it up in her fat little fist and yanked it to her mouth.

Kevin looked over at Julianne. She sighed.

"Fine. I'll call her doctor tomorrow. Oh, there you are," she said when her father returned. From inside, she could hear Gus scooting his dish around the tile floor in the kitchen. Dad waved his cell phone.

"My agent. Asking if I'd like to give the keynote speech at some family therapists' convention in Hawaii in a couple of weeks."

Julianne frowned. "Um…isn't that kind of short notice? And aren't you supposed to be on hiatus?"

"Yes to both. But they're in a bind. And since I'd been first choice—or so Margaret says," he added, smirking, "she figured she might as well see if I was game."

"You going to do it?" Julianne said, refusing to feel as though the rug was being yanked out from under her.

"I said I'd let her know tomorrow." Dad's eyes bled into hers. "It would only be for a couple of days. But if it's not okay with you—"

"Of course it's okay with me," she said brightly. "Pip and I will be fine." Kevin cleared his throat. "And besides—" beaming, now "—Kevin's here."

Her father grunted. She wasn't sure what to make of that.

Clippers at the ready, Victor moved from rosebush to rosebush in the evening cool, dead-heading spent blooms. He might not yet be up to any gardening chore involving loaded wheelbarrows or major shoveling, but this, he could do.

Just as he obviously couldn't fix his daughter's life, but at least he could give her…time. Space. A sanctuary…

Carefully straightening, he blew out a long breath. His first instinct, when he'd heard Kevin and Julianne's conversation, had been to barge outside, cut Kevin off before he could say anything that might cause his daughter more pain. But something had stopped him—from making a fool of himself, no doubt. Although he'd still felt like a fool, hearing Kevin ram home, with a single stroke, the nail Victor hadn't even come near hitting in eighteen months:

That it was up to Julie to find her new "normal." Not anybody else.

What had most stung, however, was how she'd opened up to Kevin—not only a stranger, but a stranger with the potential to hurt her even more—in a way she never had to him. Not really. But as Victor listened, sorrow—and a profound sense of helplessness—gradually swept away the spurt of irritation. He'd had no idea the puncture went that deep, that his daughter more or less believed her life was over. Let alone that she was, in effect, taking her cue from him.

On another sigh, his gaze drifted across the garden he'd so carefully nurtured, to the unused pottery studio.

A sanctuary was one thing.

A cage, however, something else entirely.

"An' jus' where do you think you're goin'?" Felix yelled from across the shop.

"It's this strange custom we have back East," Kevin lobbed back. "Called lunch? Which for most people in this time zone ended at least an hour ago."

From behind the industrial sewing machine, Felix swatted at him, then got to his feet and waddled to the ancient fridge, hunkered in the shadows like it was embarrassed. He yanked open the door, pulled out a grease-splotched paper bag.

"Sit your ass back down." The fridge shuddered when the door slammed shut. "Lupe made burritos yesterday. Beef and bean..." Felix rattled open the bag, peered inside, then pulled out a foil-wrapped cylinder the size of a can of spray paint. After knuckling his glasses back into place, he squinted at a label hugging the foil. "Or chicken and roasted peppers."

"Whichever one you don't want."

While Kevin cleared off a corner of the worktable, Felix unwrapped both burritos and plunked them on a paper plate, then shoved them in what had to be the prototype for the first microwave, ever. Two minutes later they were chowing down, chasing the spicy food with ice-cold Cokes as the blare of mariachi music, the whine of a trio of six-foot tall fans, completed the ambience.

Felix plucked a glob of cheese out of his mustache. "Missed you at the meetin' las' night."

"Sorry," Kevin said, yawning. "Pippa's teething or something. She's been a little pill recently. It didn't seem right leaving Julianne alone after she'd been with her all day already."

Felix shoved his glasses back into place. "I wasn't gonna say nothin', but you look beat." He took another bite of his burrito. "I take it it's not goin' so good?"

One side of Kevin's mouth lifted. *Beat* didn't even begin to cover it. Not only had he been working his butt off this past week to help Felix clear up his backlog, but his impossibly cute little girl could also be a real hellraiser. And a nocturnal hellraiser at that. Kevin had taken to calling her his little Batty Bat, after a *Sesame Street* song he'd heard way too many times one summer when he'd holed up with his second-oldest brother's three preschoolers.

"Probably not any worse than you had it when your kids were babies."

Felix shrugged. "I would'n' know. Lupe and her mother, they were the ones who got up with the kids at night. In my day the father, he was expected to make the money, keep the roof over everybody's heads and food on the table. The women took care of the kids. Today…" Chewing solemnly, he shook his head. "My girls, they even have their husbands changing diapers, can you imagine?"

Kevin let out a tired chuckle. "Things've changed, Felix. Beside, the hands-off approach probably wouldn't earn me Brownie points with Pip's grandfather."

"An' I still don' get why you think you gotta prove anythin' to him. Now everybody knows for sure you're the kid's dad, what he thinks don't matter."

A small firecracker exploded inside Kevin's gut, although whether from Felix's words or the combination of caffeine and hot peppers, Kevin wasn't sure. Although, at least the paternity issue had definitely been put to rest: Give DNA samples to lab on Monday, get results by phone two days later. Freaking amazing.

"It matters," he said quietly, masking a huge yawn with his hand, his eyes watering when he finally met Felix's skeptical gaze. "A lot. If it hadn't 'a been for Victor intervening when he found out Robyn was pregnant, no telling what shape Pippa might be in. If she would've even survived at all," he added through a tight throat. "Yeah, okay," he said at Felix's snort, "so the dude's keeping her a secret was wrong. And I'm not sayin' I'm ready to forgive him for that. But love sometimes makes people do stupid stuff. And whatever else might be going on inside Victor Booth's head, he definitely loves his granddaughter."

"So you're killin' yourself to impress this *hombre?*"

Actually, he was killing himself to give Julianne a break, but there was one road he was determined to keep barricaded at all costs. Although several nights' sleep had gone a long way toward alleviating her death-warmed-over look, it hadn't done a damn thing to keep the sadness in her eyes from coming back to roost like a homing pigeon. A sadness Kevin knew better than to even think about trying to chase off.

Maybe she was right, maybe you only got one shot at true love. Or maybe some people only got one shot, and Julianne was in that group. What did he know? Not that it mattered to him, one way or the other—it wasn't like he was exactly in the market for a relationship. And certainly not with his child's aunt. Even if she hadn't been from a different planet. But if the debacle with Robyn had taught him anything, it was that he was no good at saving people, at putting himself in the middle of things he didn't fully understand.

Shoving aside something that felt an awful lot like defeat, Kevin looked at Felix. "Victor fought for that baby. And for Robyn, too, as much as he could. Now that Robyn's gone…all

I'm sayin' is, I'd like to make this as painless as possible for everybody."

"So you're gonna stick aroun'?"

Kevin pushed out a breath. "I'm putting out feelers, dropping off applications with builders, but..." He shook his head. "With the slump in new housing construction, there's lots of really good people looking for refurbishing work already. People with connections I don't have."

"Yeah, I know," Felix said. "I got some nephews in the same situation. It sucks. But you know," he said, jabbing half a burrito in Kevin's direction, "you got a job here, long as you want."

"And *you* know once Orlando gets back, there won't be enough work to keep both of us busy. Besides, much as I'm grateful—"

"Recovering people's old furniture don' exactly fire your jets."

"Not really, no. Sorry."

Felix gave him one of his long, assessing looks, then crushed his soda can and lobbed it at the garbage bin. "It jus' seems like there should be some way to work this out so nobody's hurt, you know?"

Yeah. Tell him about it.

"Okay," Felix said, picking chicken out of his teeth. "I'm not payin' you to sit around on your butt all day and eat my wife's food. The Munoz dining chairs ready yet?"

Kevin yawned again. Instead of feeling revived, lunch had only relaxed him. A nice, two-hour siesta sounded perfect right about now. "Almost. Three more seats to go and I'm done."

"Good. 'Cause this morning, she calls me all hot an' bothered, she needs 'em for a dinner party tomorrow night. Not that she bothers to tell me this before now," Felix added with a not-my-problem shrug. "But she's a good customer, so I smile and tell her, sure, no problem. Anyway, so you take 'em over there when you're done, okay? Then go home. Get some sleep, for godssake."

"You kicking me out?"

"Before you keel over an' break somethin'? Damn straight."

Two hours later, chairs delivered and Mrs. Munoz's check for the balance safely tucked in his back pocket, Kevin let himself into Victor's house. As usual, Gus greeted him, making up in sincerity what the ancient pooch lacked in energy, and Kevin thought how nice it would be—as he spotted Mia's wedding invitation on the hall table—to have a house and a dog and a wife to go with the kid.

"Leave it to me," he said to the dog, who cocked his head at him, "to do everything bass-ackward, right?" The dog swiped his tongue across Kevin's knuckles, sympathetic but fresh out of advice.

The house was quiet and cool and spotless, smelling of Pledge and Windex—the Merry Maids had already been there when he'd left that morning. Robyn had told him—with accompanying eye rolls—that there'd been various housekeepers when they'd been kids. But Victor had never bothered to replace the last one, who'd quit when Robyn was still in high school. Now, as Kevin stood in the tiled vestibule, listening to the Gus's happy panting, the soft ticking of the grandfather clock by the stairs, he almost recoiled from the mustiness of disappointment and heartache permeating the air.

The loneliness lurking in the corners, waiting to pounce on whoever set foot inside.

The hell with that, he thought, striding to the kitchen for a glass of iced tea, his mood lifting slightly when he saw the box of baby cereal, a little feeding dish and spoon lying on the counter. Julianne had been almost sheepish when she'd told him the doctor said of course they could try feeding Pippa solids, that her interest in their food was a definite sign that she might be ready. Especially since she probably wasn't going to be a delicate little thing.

As he chugged his tea, his gaze landed on one of the cabinets.

Victor was right: the wood *was* good, and in excellent shape; stripping them was definitely the best way to go. Probably wouldn't take that long, either. And they'd definitely be a piece of cake after taking off the three coats of NASA-worthy enamel in the old inn's kitchen. Man, had that been a nightmare or what?

Speaking of cake, he opened Mia's wedding invitation, frowning at the prissy script on an ivory background. This from the chick he never even saw wear makeup until after she graduated from college.

Clearly, those days were over, Kevin thought on a sigh as he grabbed his tea and headed upstairs to shower and change. As he neared Pip's room, however, he heard Julianne singing, after a fashion, to the baby. He peeked inside. The blinds were still partially drawn against the strong afternoon light, soft-edging everything in a peaceful, underwater-like glow. Julianne was sitting in the glider with Pip, her loose hair a blur of pale gold in the diffused afternoon light. Kevin instantly thought of the umpteen Madonnas his Italian grandmother had plastered all over her tiny house.

Whoa.

She was too focused on her niece to notice Kevin. In return, Pip's eyes never left Julianne's, as a small, chubby foot punched the air, a tiny hand clinging trustingly to one of Julianne's long, thin fingers, curved around the bottle.

Sure as hell this was nothing like the three-ring circuses he'd grown up with, where feeding time, no matter how old you were, almost always involved a half-dozen other people, all talking over each other. At the tops of their lungs. Nothing bothered a Vaccaro baby, boy—

"Who's my sweet girl?" Julianne cooed, wiping a trickle of formula from Pip's cheek as she sucked. Kevin thought he saw a smile flicker around the bottle's nipple, punctuated by a gurgly goo. Julianne softly laughed and shifted the baby in her lap, cocooning the two of them in their own little world. A world, Kevin thought with a stab, his presence threatened to destroy.

"How long have you been standing there?"

He started slightly, then leaned against the doorjamb, one hand halfway in his pocket. She sounded more embarrassed than ticked off. He thought. Hoped.

"Long enough."

"Spying on me?"

"Nope. Just didn't want to break the spell. Her Highness seems *much* happier today."

"Maybe because a tooth popped through."

"Really?"

"Yep. Come see."

Kevin crossed to the chair and squatted at Julianne's knees, his brain nearly shorting out from the heady combination of sweet baby and fragrant woman. "Hey, pumpkin," he said to his daughter when Julianne eased the bottle out of her mouth. "Show Daddy your new tooth...well, look at that," he said, chuckling when she grinned, revealing a tiny sliver of white on her bottom gum. "You'll be chowing down that steak any day now, won'tja?"

"Honestly," Julianne said, and Kevin grinned up at her to see she was almost grinning back. With one of those amused, tolerant looks, but still.

"Your dad out?" he said, rising again, suddenly not so tired.

"Yes," she said, getting up, as well, Pippa balanced on her hip. She was barefoot, as usual—Kevin had noticed she rarely wore shoes around the house—in a scoop-necked top and baggy shorts. Stripes of gold sunlight highlighted her jaw, her collarbone, the space where her cleavage would be if she'd had any breasts to speak of. "He was invited to a wedding anniversary party or something. Old friends. I didn't know them that well."

"Huh. I didn't think he left the house much."

"He doesn't. At least, he hasn't since I've been back. Between

Robyn, and then Pip…" She shrugged. "I don't think either of us even thought about it, to be truthful. But he didn't feel he could back out of this one," she said.

At that point lightning struck and Kevin heard himself say, "So we should do the same thing."

Julianne jumped as if that lightning had struck her. "Do what?"

"Go out," Kevin said, warming to the idea. "To eat, I mean. I doubt either of us feels like cooking. We should go to Chili's or something. Or Italian, I could really go for a meatball sub. Or Chinese, whatever. So whaddya say?"

"I don't know…" She did something weird with her mouth, then looked at him over her glasses. "So…this isn't… Never mind. Sure. Why not?"

"Well, okay. Great. Just let me hop in the shower real quick, then I'll take Pip so you can fix yourself up, and…we can go. What?" he said when Julianne sputtered a short laugh.

"So I can fix myself up?"

"You know what I mean," Kevin said, reddening. Again. "Unless you wanna go just the way you are, it makes no difference to me." His mouth pulled flat. "That didn't come out much better, did it?"

"Not really, no."

"Sorry. This is a lot harder sober. Not that there's anything *this* about it, but…" He shut his eyes. "Okay, I'm gonna shut up now."

"Sounds like a plan," Julianne said, laughing softly. "But you're right, I could definitely stand some fixing up. So here—" She plunked the baby in his arms. "You watch her first. Since it's probably going to take me a bit longer than it is you."

"It's just Chili's, for God's sake," he shouted to her as she tromped down the hall to her room. Then he looked at his daughter, sitting calmly in his arms, concentrating on some painting of flowers on the wall as she sucked on her fingers, and thought, *You should definitely laugh more often.*

And he didn't mean Pip.

Chapter Six

It was truly sad, Julianne thought as she read every single item on the menu, how long since she'd been in a restaurant. She felt as though she'd been let out on furlough.

"This is a nice place," Kevin said, gaze dreamily fixed on the gigundo TV suspended over the bar, and Julianne reminded herself this wasn't a date, it was just two lazy people in a restaurant. Even if one of those lazy people had dredged up energy from somewhere to spend forty-five minutes getting ready.

She laid aside her menu to take a sip of her water, condensation beading the outside of the tall glass, lemon wedge floating amongst the ice cubes. "I was hoping it was still like I remembered it. I haven't been here since high school."

Kevin grinned at her. "You and your gal pals useta come here to pick up guys, or what?"

"No way," she said, spreading her napkin on her lap. Blushing slightly. "The *guys* used to bring us here. Mainly for that," she said when Kevin's gaze drifted to the screen again.

"What? Oh. Sorry. You ready to order?" When she nodded, he signaled to the waitress. "But that's the Sox up there."

"Oh, yeah?"

"Yeah," he said wistfully. "Springfield's only a cuppla hours from Boston. My father useta take me to games at least three, four times every summer when I was a kid. Just me and him. Baseball's not Ma's thing...."

His gaze jerked back to Julianne's. "But don't think that means I'm gonna ignore you. Or you," he said to the baby, ba-ba-ba-ing at him from her car seat, wedged beside him in the booth. Julianne could see the occasional bootied foot pop into view, but that was about it. Kevin tickled her tummy; over a tangy ache, Julianne smiled at Pip's squeal of delight in response.

"Ma laid down the law about sports right from the start," Kevin said, his flat accent slicing through the rumble of voices around them. "You don't get so caught up in the game that you forget about everything else. Only exception is if everybody else is caught up in the game, too. Then it's okay," he said, tossing her what could be construed as a very endearing grin.

The bubbly, eager waitress appeared to take their orders. Kevin deferred to Julianne. Swiping her hair back from her face, Julianne said, "Shrimp scampi, small salad, oil and vinegar on the side." She lifted her gaze to catch Kevin looking at her—Julianne—rather...oddly.

"And you?" the waitress asked.

"Uh, yeah," he said, his eyes dropping again to the menu. "I'll have...lessee...the fried zucchini to start, then...the meatball sub—"

"Whole or half?"

"Whole. And a side order of spaghetti."

"Salad?"

"Yeah. Large. With extra ranch dressing. If I can still see the lettuce, it's not enough."

The waitress—a perky little thing probably working her way through UNM—giggled. "I could bring you a gravy boat of dressing, if you like."

"Yeah, that'd be great, thanks." After the waitress whisked away their menus—without, Julianne noticed, Kevin's eyes following—Julianne sank into the booth, letting it, and the sounds and smells of the restaurant, wrap themselves around her. Her eyes closed. "This was a good idea."

"And we don't even have the food yet," Kevin said.

Julianne "mmm'd" in response, then said, "Almost takes me back to the days before I became a complete drip."

"You think you're a drip?"

She opened one eye. "Don't you?"

"Well, I wouldn't exactly call you a party animal," he said, stuffing a piece of bread into his mouth, "but a drip? Nah."

"Thanks," she said, letting her eyes drift closed again. "I think. But God—I used to be *fun,* once upon a time."

"Somehow, I can't see you as a wild thing."

"I didn't say *wild,* I said *fun.*"

"There's a difference?"

Nice voice, Julianne decided. Soothing. Kind. She decided not to think about how he'd been her sister's boyfriend. Or whatever. "For some of us, yes."

"Do you miss it?"

She thought. "I miss…who I was then."

Kevin was quiet for so long, Julianne very nearly drifted off, even though her head was too stuffed with what her father used to call the worry worms to actually relax. She sucked in some air to wake herself up, pushing her hair out of her face again, and saw Kevin giving her another one of those odd looks. Then he said, "You look really good tonight," and it dawned on her what the odd look was. *A little slow tonight, are we?* Sheesh.

Sitting up straight, she tore off a chunk of bread from the warm, crusty loaf in the basket, dunking it into the bowl of seasoned olive oil in front of her. Okay, so she'd actually dug out her makeup and this peachy, sleeveless linen top, still in its J Jill bag…and taken the curling iron to her hair…and even put in the tiny diamond studs Dad had given her when she graduated college, but…

She couldn't decide whether to be flattered or freaked. "Really?"

"Heck, yeah. Just ask that dude over there who keeps checking you out."

"Oh, for heaven's sake," she said over a small but distinct shiver.

"You don't believe me?" Kevin said, grinning that damn grin again. He ripped off half the loaf and swished it through the oil, his eyes flicking to a spot over her shoulder. "Swear to God, the guy's been staring at you since the moment we walked in." The bread disappeared into his mouth. "Come over here to check on the baby, you can see for yourself."

"Because nothing attracts a guy like a woman with a baby," she said dryly, wondering why it was bothering her that he didn't sound even remotely jealous.

"Not to mention he obviously doesn't see me as much of a threat, either." Kevin frowned. Which, Julianne noted with an internal *hmm,* brought all sorts of planes and angles and things into much sharper focus. "Maybe I shouldn't think about that too hard," Kevin said, and Julianne thought, *That makes two of us.*

Then she smiled in spite of the hmm-ing. "As if."

Kevin pressed a hand to his chest, eyes twinkling. "I'll have you know underneath this tough-guy exterior beats the heart of a very sensitive dude."

At that, she laughed out loud, and Kevin's smile softened. "You got a great laugh, you know that? Somebody should bottle that laugh, sell it to the clinically depressed. It would snap 'em right out of it. And I'm telling you, you need to come over here. It'll be worth it, I swear."

After blinking several times to clear her head, Julianne snorted. "What is this, high school?"

"Got news for ya, sweetheart, some things never change. C'mon," he drawled. Grinning. Speaking of things that should be bottled. Or declared illegal. "I dare ya."

Finally, curiosity propelled her out of her side of the booth and over to Kevin's, where she pretended to check on Pip. Who, as it happened, was out like a light.

"Nah, you gotta lean over me…yeah, like that…so you can take a gander without him seeing you. Is he looking?"

And indeed, some guy at the bar definitely seemed to be giving her the eye. Of course he averted his gaze the moment she glanced in his direction, but in that split second she caught a glimpse of dark hair and a decent jawline.

The same split second, as it happened, that she caught a whiff of just-showered Kevin that nearly melted her panties.

And hadn't it been a dog's age since *that* had happened?

Jerking upright, Julianne scooted back to her seat, just as the waitress brought them the fried zucchini. "See?" Kevin said, diving in. "Didn't I tell ya?" He poked a zucchini stick in her direction. "Total hottie. You, I mean. Not him."

"Kevin."

"Yeah?"

"If this is your way of trying to…I don't know. Make me feel part of the human race again or something…" She considered the breaded, greasy chunks of zucchini, shuddered, then lifted her eyes to his. "Please stop. It's not necessary, for one thing. And it's making me extremely uncomfortable."

The frown again. Only this time he looked like a confused little boy. "Because I gave you a compliment?"

"Because...well, yes. Because it's too...personal."

"Nothing personal about it. I'm just stating a fact. Although if it happens to goose you into feeling good about yourself, what's the harm?"

"You think I don't feel good about myself?"

"Hey. You were the one who brought up the drip thing, not me. But..." He angled his head, as though contemplating the wisdom of whatever he was about to say, then shrugged, muttering, "What the hell?"

Only, their food arrived—Kevin's took up three-quarters of the table—so Julianne hoped the sight of sustenance might derail Kevin from whatever he'd been about to say.

"Okay," he said, attacking his spaghetti, "when you were sittin' with Pip earlier, and your hair was all messed up with the sun shining in it? You were so damn beautiful I could hardly breathe."

So much for that.

"Trick of the light," she murmured, not looking at him.

"Yeah," he said. "Except the light was comin' from someplace *inside* you."

"Brother—did you get a double dose or what?"

"What can I tell you, complimenting women was drummed into our heads from birth. See, my mother had been a circus performer—"

"You're kidding," Julianne said, garlic-scented shrimp poised inches from her mouth, thinking at this rate her brain was going to disintegrate like chewing gum in baby oil.

"Nope. She was an aerialist. One of those gals who twirl and spin and everything way up at the top of the tent?" he said, gesturing toward the ceiling with a forkful of pasta. "Of course, she gave it up when she met my father, when she was, like, nineteen. But my point is, Ma was a knockout." An affectionate chuckle preceded, "And determined to stay one to the grave. I think I was fifteen before I saw her without full makeup, and that's only because she had the flu and was too weak to lift her lipstick."

Interesting image she was getting, here. "Of course," Kevin went on, "to us kids she was just Ma, you know? But to Pops, she was a goddess. Every freaking time she'd walk into the room, he'd tell her how good she looked. If we didn't echo him, he'd pop us one on the backs of our heads. Not hard, though," he added at her horrified expression.

"Still. That's terrible!"

"Nah, that was just his way of reminding us to appreciate the effort she put into looking her best. Later on, though, I realized he'd do it as a matter of course, the same way he'd compliment her cooking or notice if she was wearing a new outfit or something." One side of his mouth lifted. "I remember overhearing him telling one of my older brothers, a woman'll put up with just about anything, as long as her man makes her feel like royalty."

"And somehow I'm not supposed to find that appalling?"

Kevin's brows drew together. "What? That paying attention to the woman in your life goes a lot further than ignoring her? That a good marriage takes effort?" His head wagged from side to side. "Maybe my father's philosophy might come across as a little, whaddyacallit—"

"Sexist?"

"I was gonna say old-fashioned. But better old-fashioned than the other end of the spectrum, right?" He leaned forward. "My parents are goin' on forty years married, they're still crazy about each other. Sure, they fight, they argue, but what they have? Solid as a rock. My three older brothers, they took their time, they picked good women, for damn sure they're gonna hang on to them. A hug, a little compliment now and then—I've seen how far that goes to making a woman who's nine months pregnant, or who just had that baby, or who feels like sludge on general principles, feel better about herself. About life. So who am I to say my father's got it wrong?"

"Kevin—"

"Come to think about it," he said, frowning at his spaghetti as he twirled it around his fork, "I'm guessing I haven't been interested in a long-term relationship before now because I'd never met anyone I thought was worth the effort. Or maybe I just wasn't ready to put forth the effort, I dunno. But I can tell you this—whoever I end up with, I fully intend to follow my father's example."

"You're going to worship your wife?"

"You got a problem with that?"

"No. But she might."

He put down his fork and looked her straight in the eye. "Your husband didn't worship you?"

It was like sitting across the booth from one of those superhero dudes who changed their personas in a flash, who would stop at nothing to right the wrongs of the world. Including, apparently, dragging the odd dead husband into the conversation. Even as Kevin glared at her, worried—and why on earth, Julianne wondered, was she finding his blatant, unapologetic machismo *attractive?*—he covered Pippa, who had sneezed in her sleep, with a receiving blanket.

"We were equals, Kevin," Julianne said at last, gaze fixed on her food. Ignoring the niggling coterie of hormones determined to make a fool out of her. "Nobody *worshipped* anybody. And amazingly enough, we were happy."

He took a bite of his sub, wiped his mouth with his napkin, then sat back, gently rocking the baby seat while he chewed. "Okay," he said at last. "Maybe *worship*'s not the word I'm going for, here. How about…honored? Or cherished? Would that work for you? You know, like love, honor and cherish?"

"Not obey?" she said, smiling in spite of herself.

"Fat chance of one of my sisters-in-law letting *that* one past," he said, and she laughed, only to feel the laugh go *poof* when he leaned forward again, once more snagging her gaze. "But just so we're clear? I'm not gonna stop giving you compliments just because it makes you feel uncomfortable."

Julianne sighed. "Doesn't that defeat the purpose?"

"Nope. The way I see it, having a hard time accepting compliments is like exercise. When you first start out, it doesn't feel natural, so you hurt like hell. So you just have to keep at it until it doesn't."

She watched him eat for a moment, then said, "You're insane."

He shrugged.

Julianne toyed with her salad for several seconds. "I guess I'm just out of practice. Accepting compliments, I mean," she said when Kevin's gaze rose to hers. "Come to think of it, Gil used to compliment me all the time, too. We complimented each other. I just never thought of it as…a tradeoff."

"Not to you, maybe," he said, grinning around a bite of his sub. When she stabbed a shrimp with her fork, he laughed. "Aw, c'mon, Julianne…tell me you weren't more disposed to, you know. Return the favor?"

She blushed. "And that's *definitely* too personal."

"Whatever. But I'm just saying, like begets like. Women may pretend it doesn't work that way, but guys know it does. But it's a win-win situation, right? Happy wife, happy husband…happy marriage. What's not to like?"

The weird thing, Julianne thought as the baby—who picked that moment to come to, bless her little heart—demanded her daddy's attention, was that Kevin's father's philosophy was actually pretty much the same as the one her own father espoused in his books. Without the implied sex-as-payoff part, of course.

But it was true. More than once when she'd come home after a horrid day at the lousy secretarial job she'd held down during her first years of marriage, feeling about as attractive as refrigerator mold, Gil would say or do something to lift her spirits, make her feel better about herself. And that in turn would put her in the mood for sex quicker than you could say, "Dinner can wait."

Not that Kevin's compliments were having the same effect, of course. It was just...interesting. From a strictly sociological perspective. That someone so different from Gil should share the same outlook on relationships.

With Pippa awake—and no longer content to sit in her seat—the rest of the meal became an endurance test as they rushed to finish, trading her back and forth to keep her distracted. Finally, while there was still a chance of their being allowed in a restaurant anywhere in Albuquerque, ever again, Kevin signaled to the waitress to pack up what was left and bring them the check.

And of course, not five minutes after they left, Pip passed out again in her car seat. It had started to rain, one of those from-out-of-nowhere downpours that would probably be over by the time they got back to the house. From the passenger seat of Julianne's Camry, Kevin twisted around to look at the baby. "Oughtta be a real trip—literally—taking her back home."

Julianne's mostly full stomach dropped as they inched through the deluge, the traffic lights like huge, blurred lollipops in the distance. "But I thought you said you were going to try to stay in Albuquerque?"

"I'm talking about going back for my sister's wedding over the holiday weekend. The folks would kill me if I don't bring the baby. You mind if I turn on the radio?"

"No, go right ahead." Amazingly, he picked an easy-rock station she actually listened to herself, from time to time. The rain let up. A little. She hesitated, then said, "You mind if I ask you a question?"

"This oughtta be good."

"I don't know about good. And it's really none of my business, but...the way you talk about your family, how close you were, the obviously great relationship you had with your father... Why—"

"Did I go off the deep end?" When she nodded, he sighed. "I s'pose there are reasons," he said, staring out the alternately dry/drenched windshield. "None of 'em particularly good. I was a lousy student, I got in with a bad crowd...the usual culprits. Mostly I was just young and stupid, thought my *life* was stupid, thought drinking and drugs would make the stupid stuff go away." Her eyes fixed on the road, Julianne sensed him looking at her. "When I think about how badly I hurt the people who loved me, it makes me sick."

All she could do was nod.

The rain cloud had indeed drained itself by the time they pulled into her father's garage. Julianne noted, with a dull ping of curiosity, that her father wasn't back yet.

His sacked-out daughter extricated from her baby seat, Kevin headed toward the door to the kitchen. "Now that the rain's stopped," he whispered as they went through, "d'you think your dad would mind if I took a dip in the pool?"

"Oh, um, no. Of course not. Go for it."

"Great." Kevin silently crossed the kitchen, the baby slumped against his chest. "I'll just put her down, then—"

"That's okay, I'll do it. You go ahead."

"I can do both, you know." He stopped, looking at her over his shoulder, the light from the hall illuminating his eyes like some cheesy film shot. And in them she saw the unsettling surety of a man who, having fought the good fight and won, wasn't particularly afraid of whatever the next challenge proved to be. "You should join me," he said, full of meaning, and somehow she figured he wasn't talking about putting the baby to bed.

"Uh, no. I shouldn't."

"I won't dunk you or anything, I promise."

She laughed. "No, it's not that. It's...everything else."

"Well, that narrows it down."

"Sorry. But you have to admit...this is weird. And please don't make me spell it out."

"Okay. I won't. But for what it's worth?" he said, continuing into the hallway "I had a good time tonight."

"So did I, actually."

When they reached the foot of the stairs, he twisted to grin at her. "You don't hafta sound quite so surprised." And she thought, sorrowfully, *This is a good man.*

"If I do, it's not because of you. In fact...thank you."

"For...?"

"For...giving me a reason to say thank you."

Kevin watched her for several seconds, then leaned over to kiss her cheek. A peck, really. Barely one step above an air kiss. And yet just that simple, soft brush of his lips brought a lump to her throat. But not of grief, she realized.

Of longing. For things she no longer had, for things she'd never have again.

"Anytime," he said, then tiptoed up the stairs to put his little girl to bed.

Victor dropped his keys onto the brass plate on the hall table, the clatter barely penetrating his fog. Bearing his empty bowl, Gus shimmy-plodded over to welcome him.

"How come nobody fed the dog?" Victor called out to the world at large as he shucked off his silk sports jacket, dropping it on a chair beside the table.

"The *dog's* trying to pull a con on you," Julianne said from the living room archway, and Gus lowered his head and slunk back to the kitchen, where they heard the bowl clunk onto the floor. Already dressed for bed in a very chaste short summer robe and nightgown, Julie smiled. "And you're home late. You have a good time?"

"They didn't serve until after eight," Victor said, giving her a quick kiss as he passed her on his way to the bar at the far end of the room. Not that there'd been anything in it harder than full-caffeine soda for more than a year. But the events of the evening had left his mouth sand dry. Even though it was stupid, feeling this blindsided when he should have realized…

He poured a cold ginger ale into a tall glass, dropped in three ice cubes, then collapsed into one corner of the leather sofa facing the window. Only when Julianne curled up on its twin opposite did it register that her hair was fluffier, her eyes more…*there*, somehow—

"You're wearing makeup," Victor said, glad for an excuse not to discuss his own evening. At least, not until he'd come to terms with certain parts of it. Like surprise guests and such.

Clearly avoiding his gaze, his daughter tugged the hem of her robe over her bent knee, then shrugged. "Kevin and I went out to eat."

Victor's glass halted halfway to his mouth. Something told him the flush in Julie's cheeks was due to more than a too-heavy hand with a makeup brush. He took a sip of his drink, settling the sweaty bottom in the palm of his hand. "Was that a good idea?"

Her mouth twisted. "Going out, or going out with Kevin?"

"The Kevin part."

"It was just dinner, Dad."

Like hell. But Victor decided he was in no shape, or mood, to make a big deal out of it. "I assume you didn't leave Gus to babysit?"

"No," Julianne said on a snuffly little laugh. "Although we might have been able to finish our dinners if we had."

Despite the tightness in his chest, Victor smiled. "Where's Kevin now?"

"Swimming, I think. At least, he said he was going to. I've

been upstairs, reading." Frowning, she picked at something on the arm of the chair. "Okay, that's a lie. I've had a book open in front of me for the past hour, but don't ask me what it's about."

Victor's daddy antennae went on full alert. "Julie...?"

She turned her frown on Victor, even though he knew he wasn't the target. "Guilt's a bitch, isn't it?"

"Care to narrow that down a bit?"

"I don't know if I can. I mean, it felt good, getting out. Acting like a normal human being. But I still don't *feel* normal. And Kevin..."

"What? Did he do or say something?"

"Chill, Dad. No. Not deliberately, anyway. It's just..." Her bottom lip disappeared between her teeth for a moment, a nervous gesture Victor hadn't seen since Julie was a child. "It's just that Kevin's not *about* to screw this up. Or decide Pip's better off with us. So I think it's fairly safe to say," she sighed out, "that our plan isn't working."

Kevin had just touched the wall at the deep end of the pool when he sensed he wasn't alone. He whipped around, slicking water off his face, the trembling glow from the pool lights making the tall, male figure standing at the edge look like something out of a fun house.

"Please tell me you're wearing swimming trunks," Victor said.

With a low chuckle, Kevin shoved off the smooth tiles, propelling himself toward the ladder. "Not to worry," he said, hoisting himself out of the water to grab a towel from a nearby chaise. He took a half-assed swipe at his face and shoulders, knotted the towel around his waist. In the humidity left in the wake of the brief storm, the air pulsed with the sweet-spicy scents of Spanish broom, roses, petunias. The smoky tang from a late-night barbecue, several yards over. "Wouldn't want to scandalize the neighbors."

"Not that anyone could see, anyway."

"No, I guess not," Kevin said, glancing at the vine-choked privacy fence before refocusing on Victor, dressed in a dark, open-collared shirt, light-colored pants. "How was your night out?"

A moment's hesitation preceded, "Fine. How was yours?"

Kevin blew a soft laugh through his nose, then dropped into a nearby chair. "Talked to Julianne already, didja?"

Victor hesitated, then sat, as well, a few feet away. "How'd you do it?"

"Do what?"

"Get her to go out?"

"I asked her?"

Kevin couldn't quite read Victor's expression in the weird light. After a moment, though, the older man released a breath. "For months I've been trying to get her to venture farther than the supermarket or Target, or those walks she takes with Pip. Then you come along..." He looked at Kevin again. "Damn."

"Is that a thank-you *damn* or a you-better-watch-your-step *damn?*"

"I haven't decided yet."

A trickle of water snaked down the back of Kevin's neck. He wiped it off, stalling. "And like I said to Julianne—we both needed to eat, and nobody felt like cooking. So we decided to let somebody else cook for us. And maybe," he continued when Victor kept staring at him, "maybe I happened to hit her at the right moment, you know? Maybe she didn't feel comfortable hauling Pip to a restaurant before this. Or before that, she was just too sad. Somehow, I doubt her change of heart had anything to do with me."

Victor turned away. "So. You like to swim?"

Thinking, *Whatever,* Kevin said, "I was on my high school swim team, actually. For a while, anyway. Might've even made varsity if I hadn't gotten busted."

"Drugs?"

"Yup. Not only was I dumb enough to do the stuff, I was too dumb to know just how long weed stays in your pee."

Victor crossed his arms. "You don't even try to cover it up, do you?"

"What would be the point? It's not exactly a secret."

After several moments Victor said, "Do you miss it?"

"Swimming?"

Kevin heard the almost-laugh. "No."

The towel ditched, Kevin pushed back into the chair and stretched out his legs, his hands linked over his bare stomach. "Do I get cravings now and then? Yeah. Do I miss who I was then?" He twisted his neck to look at Victor. "No."

Julianne's father was quiet for a moment. "I'm sorry to keep beating this particular dead horse. But I have to be sure. That you're…"

"Not going to fall off the wagon? Hell, I'm the last person you need to apologize to. I know I went a little nuts the day we met, but when I found out I had a kid…" He shook his head. "I'd been kicked, hard, and I was kicking back. But we're in the same club now, you and me. We both see things from the same angle." He paused. "We both love our daughters and would do anything to protect them. So you go ahead and beat that dead horse all you want." The cool metal of the chair bit into his neck when he leaned back. "It can't hurt me, and sure as hell it can't hurt the horse anymore."

A moment passed before Victor said, very quietly, "It's not the horse I'm worried about getting hurt."

He met the older man's gaze. "I know," he said. "And I understand. But trust me, you've got nothing to worry about."

"You're sure of that?"

Looking back over the pool, Kevin snorted out a dry laugh. "Right now I'm in no position to hook up with anybody, okay? Or lead anybody into thinking I am. And Julianne…"

Julianne. His Lady of the Perpetual Frown. He'd finally given up fighting his attraction to her, even if he knew acting on that attraction would rank right up there with smoking pot the night before a swim meet. But damn it all, if there was just some way to set free the real woman he could see peeking out from that mountain of baggage—

Not your job, bro, he thought, followed by, *Then whose is it, huh?*

He looked at Victor. "Whether her heart ever heals again or not, I couldn't tell ya. But if it does, I sincerely doubt she'd give it up for somebody like me."

"No," Victor pushed out as he got up. "You're probably right."

Long after the patio door whooshed shut behind him, Kevin stayed put, staring at the shivery, underlit water, mentally fighting off all the old enemies who would drag him back down into hell in the name of "easing his pain." The good news was, he wasn't even remotely interested in listening to them.

The bad news was, the pain hurt like a bitch.

Chapter Seven

"I sold the house."

Victor glanced up from his computer, trying to focus on the strange combination of relief and regret on his daughter's face. He rarely worked after dinner, but he wanted to get down an idea for his upcoming speech before it slipped away. Which unfortunately tended to happen much too often these days. Now, through the haze of being interrupted, her words finally registered. "You did what?"

"Sold the house," she repeated. Spindly limbed as a marionette in her shorts and loose top, Julianne crossed the office's Kilim carpet to sit cross-legged on the window seat overlooking the backyard. "Allie and Peter have been at me for months to sell it to them, so—" she shrugged, absently rubbing her elbow "—I did. Since it's pretty obvious I'm not going back to Seattle."

Makeupless, her hair pulled into a ponytail, she reminded Victor of her teenage self. Except, the teenage Julianne would have bounced into his office and flopped down in a chair to launch into some outlandish tale, usually attended with much hand waving and eye rolling. And giggling.

Even after all this time, he barely recognized the solemn, life-weary woman sitting in front of him. Victor's heart cramped, wanting the giggly teenager back. Or at least the giggles, which with maturity had mellowed into a lovely, musical laughter. He sometimes almost heard it when she was with Pippa, but it seemed hollow, somehow, like the melody line of a piano piece without the richness of the bass line underneath.

"I think you did the right thing."

Her lips barely curved. "I do, too."

But the regret was in no hurry to pack its bags. Not that Victor entirely blamed her—he'd visited Gil and her a few times in the funky little house overlooking Puget Sound, its backyard a series of deep terraces smothered in flowering bushes and perennials. She'd had no trouble finding renters, friends who, according to her, had always loved the place as much as she did.

"Allie's pregnant," she said quietly. Dry-eyed. "The house will be perfect for them."

Just cry, dammit, Victor thought, more than a little selfishly. At least tears would have given him a signal, a clue as to what to do, to say. His own eyes stung. *Don't you dare make me resort to platitudes, young lady.*

Then she smiled and said, "Hey. I could use a hug, here," her arms already open when he reached her, and he tucked her against his chest, thinking, *I've got you, you're safe,* followed by *Who are you kidding?* After all, it wasn't as if they hadn't been down this road before.

Several times.

In those first, horrible months after Lois's death, it had sometimes been hard to tell who was comforting whom, which one was being strong for the other. Or for Robyn, even though she'd resisted both their efforts to steer her through hell. Still, Victor had believed—because he'd had to, otherwise he'd have gone insane—that the hell was temporary, that eventually they'd all move on with their lives. And Julianne had: She'd gone on to college, met Gil, gotten married, moved to Seattle. Had almost launched a business.

Done everything in her power to start a family to fill her wonderful little house, Victor thought with a prick to his heart.

And he, too, had done his best to follow his own advice. He'd dated from time to time, once seriously. Very seriously, in fact. Until Beth moved to northern Virginia to be closer to her son, who worked at the Pentagon, and her grandchildren. She'd asked Victor to come with her. Pleaded, actually. But with Robyn the way she'd been…

He hadn't dated since. Hadn't wanted to.

Then he'd walked through the Sheltons' front door the other evening to find Beth in their living room, luscious in a flowing orange dress that showed off her freckled shoulders and collarbone. A glass of wine in her hand, her half-silver hair haphazardly bunched on top of her head, she'd beamed. Pleased. Wary.

"No, I'm just here for the party," she'd said when they finally snatched a moment alone, her soft brown eyes wistful. Then she'd smiled again, giving the laugh lines free rein over a face enhanced by nothing except the joy of being alive. "Since I introduced Annie and Mel, I'm apparently responsible for the last thirty-five years of their lives."

As they had introduced the widowed Beth to Victor, five years before.

"The offer still stands, by the way," she'd said later, when she'd walked him out to his car, wrapped her long arms around his waist, gently touched her mouth to his. And he'd held her, torn, and said, "And I still can't," because he knew Julie still needed him. That his duty as a father came first.

"I understand," Beth had said, and Victor had wondered at the resilience of the human heart, how much abuse it could take and still beat.

Now here he and Julie were, again holding each other up, refusing to acknowledge the loneliness reflected in the other's eyes. Or the dread, that in a few weeks Pip might be gone and all they'd have would be each other.

Victor seriously doubted this was how Julianne had imagined her life, the spinster daughter caring for her elderly father. Not that he was anywhere nearly elderly. Nor was Julianne a spinster. But the way things were going—

"Oh…sorry," Kevin said from the doorway, Pippa balanced on one hip. Julianne pulled away, straightened, as Kevin made more apologetic noises.

"No, it's okay," Julianne said, brave-faced.

"But you're not," he said, with somewhat the same face, and Julie stuck out her chin and said, "I'm fine," and Victor didn't know what to make of any of it.

Especially of Kevin.

Not that the kid's—his mouth pulled tight as he thought, *Man, not kid*—heart wasn't in the right place. He was certainly good with the baby, pulled his weight around the house, seemed more than sincere about turning his life around. But despite his assurances the other night, whenever Victor saw Kevin and Julianne in the same room every hackle he owned sprang to attention, because she was lonely and vulnerable and Kevin was a good-looking young man with probably enough testosterone for an entire tribe, and the whole thing with Pippa was impossibly complicated and nobody knew better than Victor the dangerous places that complicated led to.

"I sold my house in Seattle, that's all," Julianne said, taking the baby from Kevin, who frowned. Seeing far more than Victor wanted him to see.

"That must've been hard," he said, confirming it.

"Not really," Julie said, and Victor thought, *Liar,* as Julie held Pippa up, smiling into her eyes. The baby grinned back, a last beam of sunlight catching on a silvery thread of drool.

"Hey, little girl—ready for your evening stroll?"

"Mind if I come along?" Kevin said, and Victor coughed, diverting Julie's attention fast enough to catch the glimmer of ambivalence in her eyes.

Don't, he silently pleaded, not trusting the loneliness or the vulnerability and especially not the hormones, which he strongly suspected were prancing impatiently like race horses at the starting gate. Because one day she was going to wake up, like Sleeping Beauty, and realize what she'd been missing. Her brows lifted. As did the corners of her mouth, nudging aside the ambivalence.

"Of course I don't mind," she said to Kevin—who actually looked a little surprised, truth be told—but not before shooting Victor a look that clearly said *Silly old dear.*

That Sleeping Beauty was already awakening.

Oh, Julie, Victor thought. *Julie, Julie, Julie.* He'd no sooner get a handle on what she was feeling than she'd do a complete one-eighty on him. He hadn't missed her coolness around Kevin since their evening out—a coolness brought about by nervousness, he'd bet. So why the sudden change of heart? Why the *Dad. Please. I'm a big girl* warning look?

A look he'd seen more times that he could count in his *younger* daughter's eyes. Robyn had been the quixotic one, the daughter who'd change her mind on a dime, just to rattle his chain. Not Julie. Not his rock.

What *was* this? *Who* was this?

After they left—without, Victor noted, inviting him along—

he felt as though someone had reordered the cosmos and forgotten to tell him.

And that he hadn't felt this alarmed since that ridiculously shaggy boy from Julie's English class had come to take her out when she was sixteen.

They'd been walking for ten minutes or so, not saying much. Which gave Julianne ample opportunity to argue with the stinky old monster inside her head doing its best to convince her she was absolutely petrified.

Of what? she asked herself, only to accidentally bump into Kevin when they stepped off a curb and she momentarily lost her balance and his fingers closed around her elbow, steadying her, and she thought, *That's what.*

At least, she thought that's what she'd thought. Hard to tell over the whump-whumping of her heart. Because ever since that seemingly innocent dinner, all those memories of Gil that had so scared the bejeebers out of her had begun to cede the floor to thoughts about Kevin. Talk about bejeebers. Yeesh. Because what the hell was she supposed to do about *that?* About him? About—

"You okay?" he asked.

"Of course I'm okay," she said, huffy, although because he'd asked or because she was annoyed with herself for stumbling, she couldn't say. Kevin chuckled softly, clearly one of those men unaffected by huffiness. She glanced over at him. Naturally, he'd taken the stroller handles the minute they'd gotten outside, even though they were set for her height, not his, so he had to hunch over slightly as they walked. The last rays of the sunset licked at his jaw and cheekbones, and she reminded herself that it was the Devil's ability to make himself appealing that caused *soooo* many people to crash and burn—

Brother. Her thoughts were streaking around inside her head like a bunch of greased pigs.

"Any news on the job front?" she asked, grabbing one by the foot as it sailed past.

He snorted. "I've put in applications with pretty much every contractor in the Rio Grande Valley."

"And?"

"And...I've got a couple of maybes." She heard the frustration in his voice. "Nobody seems to be looking for foremen, though."

"You can do that?"

"I have done that. Just not here." He steered the stroller around a cottonwood root eruption in the sidewalk. "I'm not completely without skills, Julianne," he said quietly. "It's not like I spent the past ten years wasted 24/7." He leaned forward to touch Pippa's head as they walked. "And it's not like I'm too proud to take whatever I can find. But it'd be nice to be able to afford better than some crap apartment. Maybe even a house. So there'd be a backyard for Pip."

Julianne felt as though she were imploding. "I'm so sorry."

Kevin glanced at her, frowning. "For what?"

"For sometimes forgetting what this must be like for you, trying to make all the pieces fit. You didn't exactly ask for this."

"I didn't exactly go out of my way to prevent it, either," he said after a moment.

"Still. You're dealing with it."

"Aside from the occasional 'Oh, hell, what now?' moment, you mean?"

"For goodness' sake, Kevin—everybody has those! *Not* everybody gets past them. Why do you think I admire you so much?"

Blushing, she yanked her head front again just as Kevin said, "Considering how you've been avoiding me the past cuppla days, that's not exactly the vibe I was getting."

"Avoiding you? Don't be ridiculous. You're here now, aren't you?"

"But 'why' is the question. I mean, here I thought we'd gotten along so well at dinner, but..." He pushed out an obviously fake sigh, then slammed a forearm across his eyes. "And I sat by my phone, waiting and *waiting* for your call..."

"You nut," she muttered. Still blushing. Chuckling, Kevin lowered his arm.

Some guy started up his lawn mower, obliterating conversation for a half block. At last Kevin said, "I just wasn't aware that thank-yous could be rescinded."

Julianne grabbed for another piggy, but it squealed and slipped out of her grasp. "It wasn't. I just... Never mind. Anyway...you could have walked away without a second thought, knowing Pip would be taken care of. Dad and I had offered you the easiest out in history. Which you didn't take. Only an idiot wouldn't admire that."

"Or your father."

"Dad'll come around," she said, over a sudden barrage of ba-ba-bas from the stroller. "In fact," she said in response to—or in spite of—Kevin's snort, "I suppose...you could continue living with us. If push came to shove."

"Uh...no. Thank you."

"Why not?"

"Because it's weird. Because...I can't imagine you'd be happy with that."

"I'd manage," she said curtly, letting more piggies slip past. "You have to admit it would be convenient. And it's not as if we don't have the room—"

"And maybe Victor has to accept that I'm Pip's father, but he obviously still hasn't forgiven me for getting Robyn pregnant in the first place. If you ask me, I think he's got some serious mixed feelings about me being around at all, even temporarily. For the long haul?" He shook his head. "No damn way."

"He's actually said that to you?"

"He doesn't have to. I can feel what he's thinking every time he looks at me." He paused. "Especially since he's worried I'll take advantage of you."

"Of *me?* You're not serious!"

"Ask him yourself if you don't believe me."

"But...but that's absurd!"

"I know. In fact," Kevin said, his eyes straight ahead, "I told him, flat-out, that he had absolutely nothing to worry about."

"So...what's the problem?" Julianne said, feeling oddly deflated.

"That one's easy. He doesn't trust me."

Julianne dared to glance at Kevin's profile, but for once he was absolutely expressionless. "So you have to earn his trust."

"What the hell do you think I've been trying to do the past two weeks?"

She had nothing to say to that.

"So," Kevin said, ambling along. "What're you gonna do now that you sold your house? Stay with your dad indefinitely?"

Although Julianne really wanted to say, *What's it to ya?* she settled for, "It seems kind of silly for Dad and me to have separate places when the house is more than large enough for us both. Think of the energy we'll save."

"Ah. So this is an environmental decision."

"Would that work for you?"

He grinned over at her. "Like hell," he said, and she thought, *Do* not *grin like that at me. Ever.* "I gather your father's really attached to the house."

As far as skirting away from dangerous subjects went, it wasn't great, but she'd take it. "His parents built it new in the fifties, when he was still a kid. He's lived there nearly his entire life."

"Even when he was doing the morning show out of New York?"

"He wasn't actually in the studio that much, so he stayed with friends when he was there. But most of his segments were filmed here." Her mouth thinned. "I know it probably seems strange, why Dad would want to stay someplace with so many unhappy memories. But there were lots of good ones, too. Granna and Gramps were wonderful. Big-hearted. Funny as hell. They're both gone now, of course. But they lived with us—or we with them, I guess—when I was little. And I was married there..." She went quiet.

"Sorry."

"For what?" she said, irritated. "A wedding went a long way toward erasing the bad memories. And yes, I know, that wasn't the end of it. But that wasn't the *house's* fault, was it?"

"No," he said quietly. "I don't suppose so."

"I know it's dumb, thinking of the place as some sort of safe haven, but at the moment, it is. Besides, Dad needs me, too. At least I feel...useful."

"But what about your own life?"

"You just don't get it, do you? This *is* my life. And believe it or not, I'm perfectly okay with it."

"If you say so."

"I am, dammit!"

"A little louder, honey—they didn't hear you in Santa Fe."

"My God, you're insufferable!"

"And that's the most animated I've seen you since I got here."

She stopped dead in her tracks. "What?" she said to his back.

"When I first met you, you were practically a zombie," he said over his shoulder, as smoky blues and teals snuffed out the remnants of the brilliant sunset. "If that was you bein' okay, I shudder to think what *not* okay looked like."

Julianne's sandals slapped the sidewalk as she scurried to catch up to him. "You deliberately goaded me."

"Didn't take much, did it? Look," he said more gently, coming to a stop, "I'm not belittling how ya feel, believe me. I know things've been rough. But it kills me to see anybody get stuck in the dead zone, okay?" His gaze caressing hers, he took a deep breath, then letting it out, "And these days, I can't just turn my back. Pretend it's not my problem."

Like I did with Robyn, she read in his eyes, flooded with both remorse and determination. "I was there, Julianne. So I know how much it sucks. And that once you're in it, sometimes—often—it just seems easier to stay there than kick yourself in the butt to get out. And—"

"What?"

"You'll hit me if I tell you."

"I'll hit you if you don't. What?"

He started walking again. "It's just...when you get all prickly—"

"I do not!"

"Yeah, you do. Not all the time, no, but it's like being in a minefield. Everything's goin' good, then suddenly...*boom.* Except as I was *tryin'* to say...when that happens, it's like you're wearing somebody else's clothes." He glanced at her, then front again. "Like that's not the real Julianne."

"Kind of a leap for someone who doesn't even know me, don't you think?" she said, sounding prickly.

"You weren't prickly when we went out to eat. But you sure as hell have been since. Not with Pip or your father, though. Just with me."

"That's because you confuse me," she said, immediately wishing she hadn't.

A very loud, very close cricket started up. "In what way?"

"I don't *know,*" Julianne said, thinking, *How do I get myself into these things?* "That's why I'm confused. And anyway, it's not actually that *you* confuse me as much as..." She shut her eyes; the piggies faced her, smiling their smarmy little piggy smiles, daring her. *Scram,* she thought, then opened her eyes again and looked at Kevin. "Your being around has just brought a lot of stuff to the surface. Stuff I don't know what to do with. Like when I had to clean out my grandmother's closets after she died. Only this time, it's my own brain."

They'd walked past two more houses before Kevin said, "You're not saying anything I hadn't already figured out. But dammit, Julianne—whatever your father's issues, whatever *your* issues—we need to at least be friends, doncha think? For Pippa's sake. Right now I'm getting along better with Victor than I am you, and that's buggin' the hell out of me."

Julianne opened her mouth, only to shut it again. Because the whole situation was bugging the hell out of her, too. She was feeling a bit Jekyll and Hyde-ish these days. And she had not Clue One what to do about it.

"I'm trying my best here, honey," Kevin said quietly beside her.

"I know you are," she said sadly, then added, "So am I."

Nobody said anything for the rest of the walk.

"Of course," Kevin said on the phone to his brother as he watched Julianne through his bedroom window, playing with Pip on a beach towel, "if you absolutely can't bear the thought of being without your daughter for a few days…"

"Are you kidding?" Rudy Vaccaro said. "I'd send her on a plane tonight, if I could. The kid's got wedding fever far worse than our sister. She's about to drive all of us nuts. But she's also promised Mia she'd go down there and help her out for a few days before the big event. That pretty much trumps goin' cross country to hang out with her uncle."

"I guess so," Kevin said, smiling despite the heaviness that continually threatened his good mood, like the disorganized globs of marshmallowlike clouds periodically blotting out the sun. Julianne was wearing one of those tankini things that basically left everything to the imagination, except for her legs, which were so white they glowed. The suit was blue. Or green. Or blue-green—

"So. Your work with Felix is done?" Rudy asked, as Kevin leaned left to watch Julianne and the baby when they moved out of sight.

"Yeah," Kevin sighed out. "I've got some prospects lined up, but nothing to knock anybody's socks off. There's one outfit that specializes in flipping fixer-uppers. They sounded pretty promising when I talked to them yesterday."

"But…?"

"But nothing. It's honest work, the pay's fair if not great, and it's here."

After a moment, Rudy said, "You'll never guess who stayed with us last weekend."

"Okay, I'll bite. Who?"

"Sandy Epstein. Big TV-network exec. Mia handled his daughter's bat mitzvah party a cuppla months ago. He mentioned as how he and his wife were looking for a weekend getaway. Mia recommended the inn. Really nice people, him and his wife, both. You'd like 'em. And Stace and their girl got on like gangbusters. Anyway, for reasons known only to Violet, she's put these before-and-after pictures of the inn up in the lobby. So I see this guy looking the place over but good, right? Examining every detail. And the second night he's here, he takes me aside, asks me who did the renovation. So I tell him you did."

"Uh…*we* did, Rudy. You and me. And Vi."

"Yeah, we did the grunt work, but we were just following your instructions. You're the one who knew the hell what you were doing. How to restore the woodwork and molding and all that. Anyway, so Epstein asks me if you're available."

Kevin switched his phone to his other ear. "Available? For what?"

"Seems he just bought this big old place in Connecticut. Not far from Mia's and Grant's, actually. But apparently it needs work. A lotta work, from what he's saying. And he's looking to put together a crew to start work in a month or so, after closing." Rudy paused. "So I gave him your cell number."

"You did *what?* Rudy—what are ya talkin' about?"

"I'm talkin' about, this guy said he's been interviewing all sorts of people, but he says you've got the 'sensitivity' or something he's lookin' for. It's a big project, we're probably talking several months. And once you get your toe in back here..." He could practically see his big—and he meant *big*—brother shrug. "It's right up your alley, right? And who knows where it could lead."

"Yeah, but..." He pushed out a pained sigh. "I more or less told Victor and Julianne I'd stick around."

"You also said that depended on what kind of work you found out there. You know as well as I do the big bucks the better rehabbers pull in back here. So you'll talk to the guy when he calls?"

"Of course I'll *talk* to the guy, but..." Kevin rubbed the space between his brows hard enough to remove the top two layers of skin, then released another breath. "I made a promise, Rudy. A promise to two people I don't dare screw around on, okay? Besides, I can't believe this Epstein dude wouldn't be able to find somebody else with far better qualifications than me. The area's crawling with renovation experts. And, anyway, once he finds out about my background—"

"He already knows about your background, Kev. He's got a brother went through the same thing. He understands. And he told me to pass along his congratulations for making it past a year. Anyway...so you talk to him, see what he has to say. I already apprised him of your situation, but you never know, right? These things have a way of working out in ways we couldn'ta ever predicted," he said in that smug way of a man who's got everything he ever wanted. Finally.

But the more Kevin thought about it after he hung up, the more he realized that the likelihood of this Sandy Epstein calling him was slim to none. Although he had to admit the idea of getting his hands on one of those big old Connecticut houses made him salivate. Restoring Rudy's old inn had really gotten his juices going; he'd loved stripping the old girl bare, then dolling her back up again. Kinky as that sounded, Kevin thought with a chuckle. Replacing stained wall-to-wall carpet and outdated bathroom fixtures in seventies three-bedroom ranches just didn't hold the same allure.

But as he'd said to his brother, he thought as he changed into his swimming trunks and grabbed a towel, it was honest work. And Kevin was in no position to gripe about it not exactly being a dream job.

When he pushed open the patio door, Julianne was slowly fording the shallow end of the pool, occasionally dipping Pip's chubby little legs into the water. Each time, the baby let out a squeal, her feet sending diamond-drops of water flying, and Kevin could practically hear her thinking, *Now this is more like it!* A picture popped into his head, of him sitting in the bleachers by the high school pool, the steamy air smelling of chlorine, cheering himself hoarse for a teenage Pip churning the pool water into foam as she streaked past her opponents in the hundred-meter freestyle.

But where, he wondered, would that high school be?

And would he be sitting there alone, or…?

"Now there's a serious face," Julianne said, squinting up at him, that damned wariness in her gaze forcing Kevin's to the baby. Who, he now saw, was wearing a tiny ruffled one-piece in a blinding shade of pink. And a floppy, broad-brimmed hat that grazed Julianne's water-flecked chest as she held her close.

Kevin lowered himself into the pool, reached for his daughter. After a hesitation so slight Kevin might have almost imagined it, Julianne passed her to him. In the process, hands touched, wet skin slicked over wet skin, gazes were averted…and Kevin swallowed a sigh.

"Just projecting into the future," he said mildly, dipping and gliding backward, careful to keep the baby's face out of the water. When he noticed Julianne's raised brows, he grinned. "About Pip. The way she reacted the first time I gave her a bath? Shoulda known we had a little fish on our hands."

Her hand tented over her eyes, Julianne gave him a funny look. At the "we" in that sentence, probably. Kevin mentally slapped himself, remembering the note they'd ended their walk on the other night. And as he continued swishing his little girl through the sun-heated water, one of those clouds momentarily smothered the sun…and the heaviness got heavier, as he realized that going through the motions of doing the "right" thing—whatever that turned out to be—would never be enough. For any of them.

"I owe you an apology," she said, interrupting his thoughts.

Again finding purchase on the pool bottom, Kevin frowned at her. "For what?" he asked, just as the sun popped back out.

The water glittered as she skimmed her palms across the surface, not looking at him. Drops dotted her shoulders, lazily trailed down her neck, like jewels. Finally she lifted slightly unfocused eyes to his—she wasn't wearing either her glasses or contacts, he realized. "For forgetting that this isn't about me. It's about Pippa. And you're right. For her sake we need to be friends."

He could see her pulse at the base of her throat. The borderline terror in those pale, myopic eyes.

"You're sure?"

"I'm sure," she said, and he thought, *Like hell.*

Chapter Eight

A gal can only endure so many sleepless nights before admitting she's wrong.

In Julianne's case that meant—no matter what arrangements they ultimately worked out about Pippa—keeping Kevin at arm's length wasn't going to work. The abject terror that prospect provoked notwithstanding. But it wasn't his fault that watching him with Pip made her one miserable chickie, stirring up all those aborted hopes and dreams about her and Gil raising a child together.

It wasn't Kevin's fault that watching him blossom into someone she couldn't have made her heart hurt.

The combination of sun and water heightened his scent, his Kevin-ness, exploding a small, sharp sting of awareness in her midsection. He was looking at her, frowning slightly, his firm mouth drawing her gaze like a magnet.

She swam a little away, then turned back, lazily treading the water in the deep end. "So is your niece coming out?" she called to him.

Kevin shook his head, then glided in the other direction. Pip giggled. "No. My sister has dibs. For her wedding?" he reminded her.

"That's too bad," she said. "I would have liked to meet her."

"Maybe you will someday."

"Maybe," Julianne said, then dived underneath the surface, the cool water practically sizzling against her heated skin.

On Saturday morning Pip woke up at her usual ungodly hour. Except this time her daddy was two steps ahead of her. "Hey, gorgeous," Kevin said, plucking her out of her crib to change her soggy diaper, "whaddya say we have some breakfast, and then you and me can start in on a big surprise for your grandpa? I'll start in, anyway. You can watch. How's that?"

On her back on the changing table, Pippa pressed her lips together and blew a great big baby raspberry.

"Yeah, you're gonna fit into this family just fine," Kevin said, wiping his face. "And don't you dare laugh." So instead, her eyes got wide, her mouth pursed into a perfect little *O*, and her legs pumped as if she was on one of those Nautilus exercise machines. Then she laughed.

Chuckling himself, Kevin carted her down to the kitchen, let Gus out back to do his business, fed the kid, cleaned the kid, burped the kid, set the kid into a baby seat with a bunch of brightly colored crap hanging over it and glowered at the cabinets.

"You're goin' *down*," he said, and started emptying the first one, carting the stuff out to the dining room.

A half hour later Victor's flabbergasted, "What on earth are you doing?" brought a smile to Kevin's face. He lowered the cabinet door he'd just removed to the kitchen floor, then turned to Julianne's father, who was dressed in his usual loose-fitting short-sleeved shirt, khakis, sandals. "It's usually easier to remove the doors before you strip 'em. You got a sander by any chance? The gunk should take care of most of the stain with no problems, but a sander'll take care of any stubborn residue." He scratched his neck. "And I just put on coffee, in case you're interested."

Victor blinked a couple of times before he said, "I didn't ask you to do this."

"I know. But it needs doin', right? Unless you changed your mind…?"

"No, no, I haven't changed my mind. It's just…" The older man's brows pushed together. "Why?"

Kevin popped out the next hinge nail with a mallet and screwdriver, caught the door before it fell on his head and grinned. "I think it's called kissing up."

Victor gawked at him for a second or two, then let out a short laugh. "You're too much."

"Actually, I'd settle for just being *enough.* That's all I'm trying to prove here, Victor. That I'm enough."

Julianne's father crossed to the coffeemaker and poured himself a cup. "For whom?"

"For you, obviously. But for Julianne, too." Behind him, dead silence. Kevin sighed. "It's like I told her, if we're gonna make this work between us—about Pippa, I mean—being friends'll make that a whole lot easier."

"Friendship can't be forced, Kevin."

"I know that. But there's such a thing as not giving it a chance, too."

On a grunt, Victor pulled a carton of half-and-half out of the fridge, poured some into his coffee. "And Julie agrees with you?"

"She had to think about it for a while. But yeah. She does." Although God knew Kevin wasn't about to mention the barely suppressed, ah, interest in Julianne's eyes the other day in the pool.

That she'd chosen to reawaken on his watch was flattering, Kevin supposed. And for her sake, he was glad. But for damn sure he wasn't dumb enough to think anything would come of it. As it were.

Convincing himself it was for the best, however—not so easy.

And if Victor had any idea what was going through Kevin's brain, he'd probably have him shot. Apparently not, however, since, after several sips of his coffee, he said, "Of course I have a sander. Several, in fact. In the garage. Workbenches, too, anything you need. But I do the actual staining, you got that?"

"Deal," Kevin said, banging loose another hinge pin.

Distractedly rubbing the dog's velvety head on his thigh, Victor watched Kevin make short order of dismantling the kitchen cabinets, all the while keeping up a one-sided conversation with Pippa, safe in her baby seat several feet away. During his years of practice, Victor had counseled far too many detached fathers—and mothers, too, for that matter—to begrudge Kevin his obvious, and completely unfeigned, affection for his child.

But neither was Victor stupid. Or too old to remember what it was like to yearn. Especially for things you weren't supposed to want. And the yearning in Kevin's eyes, his voice…the unspoken acceptance of what Victor now felt fairly certain wouldn't happen…

He sipped his coffee, thinking he might have been tempted to feel sorry for the boy, if it hadn't been his own daughter they were talking about.

Oddly enough, he trusted Kevin. At least, a helluva lot more than he'd ever thought possible two weeks ago. Integrity could sprout in the most unlikely places, he supposed. Oh, the kid was still rough around the edges—and with his background, likely to remain so—but Julianne's intuition about him had apparently been a lot more on the mark than Victor had given her credit for. Whether he'd completely shed his past, Victor couldn't say. But he was obviously trying. And he obviously loved his daughter.

Kevin's own daughter, he'd meant. But when Julianne shuffled into the room, yawning, still in her nightgown, hair uncombed, face creased, and Victor caught Kevin watching her, his expression earnest and gentle and torn, Victor inwardly sighed.

His only hope, then, was Julianne herself. That she was far too sensible to confuse loneliness with something else. Something more. Not his Julianne, who'd never even had a serious boyfriend before Gil.

Julianne, Victor thought as he finished his coffee and joined her at the coffeemaker to refill his cup, he could trust not to do something stupid.

Or so he hoped with everything he had in him.

It was the grown man's equivalent of a candy store.

Tools of every type and description hung from pegboards, lay reverently on pristine metal shelves, patiently waiting to prove their worth. Hand tools, power tools, tools to make a man's hands itch to build something, fix something, leave his mark on the world. Or at least his house.

Kevin thought of Benny Vaccaro's ramshackle workshop in their basement, a conglomeration of cluttered shelves, warped benches and half-rusted tools, most of which hadn't worked in twenty years. "Go get me a hammer, wouldja?" his father would say, striking fear in the heart of whichever kid he'd snagged. "It's in the workshop, you can't miss it."

Five minutes later would come the inevitable disembodied, "Where, Pops? I don't see nothin'."

"It's right there, on the whaddyacallit, the bench. Or maybe the shelf."

"Which shelf?"

"Right by the screwdriver set," Pops would yell back. "You can't see it…?"

Smiling at the memory, Kevin scanned the neatly lettered, laminated labels on the edges of each shelf, above which sat exactly whatever the labels said. A far cry from the curling, ragged strips of masking tape that adorned the sagging wooden shelves in the Vaccaro basement, the ballpoint pen scribblings faded beyond legibility. Still, Kevin owed whatever skill he had to his father's barked instructions to measure twice, cut once…then hammer the crap out of stuff.

Needless to say, he found the sanders almost immediately. But he'd no sooner grabbed them when several sturdy, white packing boxes on the next set of shelves over caught his eye, all labeled in a large, girly print:

CATS. PLATES AND MUGS. (Blue, Purple, ass't)

DOGS (Best) MUGS.

PIGS, COWS. PLATES. SMALL.

PIGS, COWS. PLATES. LARGE. (Some chipped. Keep for pattern.)

There were probably twenty boxes in all, that he could see. And on the floor, not far from his feet, one lay open, as though inviting him to peek inside. This one, however, was labeled in the same no-nonsense block printing as the folder in the kitchen, the labels on the tool shelves:

JULIE/KITCHEN

Kevin set the sanders down on a nearby worktable and bent over the open box, unfolding the flaps to reveal several newspaper-shrouded items. Carefully he unwrapped the first one, a large, bright blue bowl around which cavorted an assortment of very fat, impossibly colored cats…in bikinis and sunglasses. With gauzy wings sprouting from their backs.

Grinning, he set the bowl aside to unwrap the next piece, this one a pitcher in the same blue, but now adorned with a droopy-eyed hound dog in a tux. And wings. A set of mugs followed in assorted bright colors, some with cats, some with dogs, some with pigs, all outlandishly costumed, all winged. And at the bottom, a large serving platter featuring a high-heeled cow wearing a tiara and pearls, her wings keeping her from actually touching the ground—

"What are you doing?" Julianne squeaked.

Swearing, Kevin caught the platter as it slipped from his fingers. "Give me a heart attack, why doncha? And the box was already open."

Now dressed in what was basically a short, olive-colored tent, Julianne waded through drifts of crumpled newspaper to get to him. "And I suppose the paper just happened to fall off all by itself, too."

"Okay, that might have had help." Still holding the cow platter, Kevin looked up at her and thought, *On you, mad is sexy as hell.* Even if the dress wasn't. "Why are you in here, anyway?"

She started, derailed. "Dad thought you might have trouble finding the sanders."

"If I was blind, maybe." When she opened her mouth, Kevin shook his head. "You can yell at me later. After I tell you how freaking hysterical this stuff is. And ask why the hell you're keeping it all packed away."

"I intend to, thank you, and none of your business."

"Huh," he said, unrepentant. "Somebody's getting too much sleep. Speaking of which…I take it Pip's down for her nap."

"Yes. And can you change a subject on a dime or what?"

"I'm a guy, it's what we do best." He paused. "Okay, it's *one* of the things we do best."

Her gaze brushed his. Yep, definitely pink cheeks. Was it fair, flirting with her?

Did he care?

In any case, Julianne squatted beside him, her hands tightly clasped over tent-shrouded knees. She smelled so good Kevin thought he'd pass out. Then he looked over at her, and his heart cracked at the apprehension pulling her mouth into a grim line. "So what is this?" he asked gently, and some of the grimness took a hike.

"My ceramics," she said. "I haven't looked at it for a while. I'd forgotten..." She giggled. Sort of. "They're really crazy, aren't they?"

"They're insane. And wicked cool, as my new sister-in-law would say. This dude, especially—" he picked up a mug with the penguin-suited hound dog "—totally rocks."

"Yeah?"

"Yeah. But what's up with the animals having wings? Are they angels?"

She tilted her chin, indignant. "If you *notice,* those aren't angel wings. No feathers?" she said when he frowned at her. "There were part of my Fairy Tails collections. T-A-I-L-S. Because they're animals, but they're fairies, too. Never mind," she muttered, like an embarrassed kid suddenly caught singing along with her favorite pop star, "it was a silly idea...."

"Are you kidding? Not that I know squat about pottery or ceramics or whatever this is, but damn, they're funny. I mean, how can you look at this—" now he picked up the cats-in-bikinis piece "—and not just feel good?"

"That was the idea," she said quietly. "At least, originally."

Thinking, *Don't ask,* he scanned the boxes stacked on the shelves. "How come there's so much of it?"

Finally Julianne picked up one of the mugs. Sturdily balanced on her haunches as she turned it over in her hands, she stroked one finger over the ballet skirt thing choking a pig's belly. "I'd been accumulating stock to do a show in Seattle," she said, her gaze steady on the mug. "Thanksgiving weekend, two years ago." She paused. "The week after the accident."

"Damn, Julianne..." She shrugged. Settling his butt on the cement floor, Kevin leaned up against the side of the workbench, his knees bent, watching her turn that mug over and over in her hands, tunneling back to a time and place she'd clearly avoided visiting for some time. "And you haven't looked at it since?"

Thin, pale shoulders lifted with her breath as she set the mug down, then inexplicably wriggled back to sit beside him. "Not really, no. I had my friend Allie pack it all up while I was in the h-hospital."

On impulse, Kevin reached for her hand; she didn't resist. In fact, she twined her fingers around his and hung on for dear life, now staring at the open box like there were snakes inside.

"Julianne?"

She shook her head.

"Julianne," Kevin repeated, squeezing her hand. "Talk."

Several beats passed before she said, "What if I don't want to talk? Maybe I'm talked out, maybe I've *talked* until I'm blue in the face—"

"But not to me. And not to put too fine a point on it, but if you're still squirreling away all this stuff, I'm thinking all those other times you talked didn't do you as much good as you thought. And don't bother gettin' all pissy on me, it won't have any effect whatsoever. Not after all the Italian women I've been around."

Silence. So he said, "I talked my head off, too, to this or that counselor or whoever, when I was goin' through rehab." He twisted enough to see her profile. "And they helped, sure. Jump-started me into thinking differently about who I was, why I was doing what I was doing. But all of those sessions put together didn't add up to one conversation with my father, or my sister, or one of my brothers. With people who actually gave a damn about me."

"You give a damn about me?"

"Duh."

That, at least, got a tiny smile. Followed by, "Why?"

"Damned if I know." When she finally laughed, he said, "This is what friends do, listen to each other. Right?"

"I suppose. It's just..." She huffed out a breath. "I'm afraid once I get started, I won't stop." Her gaze lifted to the boxes on the shelves in front of them. "And you've got cabinets to...do whatever you're going to do to them. Dad's impressed, by the way."

"Wait until I'm done. Then he can be impressed. And talk about switching subjects..." When she hesitated again, he said, "Forget about the cabinets, okay? Even if I don't get 'em done before the month's up, I'm not goin' anywhere. I can finish them later."

Their eyes met. "You're really not going anywhere?" Julianne said, hopeful, and Kevin got a little jazzed himself before he realized what she really meant was, *You're really not taking Pip away?*

"Not plannin' on it," he said, then raised his brows. "So...?"

She faced forward, her forehead creased. "I drew and painted my way through childhood. Fun stuff. Lots of color. My mother used to say—" she swallowed "—that I painted laughter." A long, slow sigh preceded, "I painted lots of laughter for Mom. To cheer her up on her bad days."

The remnants of quiet desperation in her voice, of a child determined to make her mommy better, made Kevin heartsick. "Did it help?"

"Apparently not. At least, not enough. After she died, it all changed. My work, I mean. It was as if...the light went out, leaving everything gray and colorless. I worked a lot in pencil and charcoal. Technically perfect, but boring as hell. Still, I majored in art in college, which is where I took my first pottery class. And I loved it, loved the..."

She flexed the fingers of her free hand. "The *sensuality* of it. The feel of the cool, slippery wet clay, how I had to literally become one with the piece as I worked on it. Even so, I'd make a pot, and it would say, 'Nice pot,' but it wouldn't say, 'Wow.' It would just sit there, quiet and unobtrusive. Like me. The me I'd become, anyway. Then I met Gil," she said, slipping her hand out of Kevin's.

On a slight grunt, she shifted forward to pull another piece out of the box. A spoon holder, Kevin thought, shaped like a cat, with a big, goofy grin. "He was in some of my classes. At the time he wanted to draw graphic novels, but eventually he became a cartoonist." She tapped one end of the spoon rest on her chin, frowning slightly. "It was a time in my life when I needed a cartoonist," she said, like this had just occurred to her.

"Makes sense to me," Kevin said, and she smiled.

"And I know it sounds corny, but being around him…turned the light back on. After all those months of shadows, I began to see color again. Not just see it, but hear it and breathe it and…" She blushed. "I told you it was corny."

"Corny as hell," Kevin said, shrugging. "And then?"

"And then…we'd been married for a while when Gil found some sketches I'd made, maybe for a children's book, of the cats in bikinis. Gil was doing well enough that I could quit my hellacious office job, but I hadn't quite figured out yet what I wanted to be when I grew up. And he said, 'You should put these on things people could use every day,' and I said, 'Right,' and he said, 'No, I'm serious,' and he nagged me so much I finally made a couple of samples just to shut him up. Except instead of shutting up, he sold them. Like that," she said, snapping her fingers. "I think Gil was more excited than I was. Which was the great thing about Gil, that it was never all about him."

"Yeah, it's men like that who give the rest of us poor slobs a bad name," Kevin muttered, earning another little smile.

"*Any*way," Julianne continued, "so then he came up with the wings idea, and that I should do other animals, and call it my Fairy Tail collection."

"So he was your whaddyacallit? Your muse?"

She jiggled her wedding band up and down for a second or two. "I don't know if it was so much that Gil was my muse as he dragged her out from hiding and gave her a swift kick in the butt," she said, and Kevin thought, *Being jealous of a dead guy is just plain nuts,* even as he was weirdly grateful that Julianne had had someone like that in her life. Which was even more nuts.

"Most people assumed we started with animals," she went on, "and then imagined them in clothes. It was totally the other way around. Lots of sketches on restaurant napkins. Flea markets were an absolute gold mine. And I'm not talking about overlooked treasures from people's basements."

Kevin smiled. "And the wings?"

"For the whimsy factor, of course."

"Of course. Because nothing says serious like a wingless pig in a ballet costume."

After another short laugh, Julianne got very quiet. Kevin briefly bumped her shoulder with his. Buddy-buddy-like. "Gil sounds like a really great guy."

"He was," she said simply, getting back on her knees to rewrap the pieces. "Not that he was perfect. He hogged the remote and absolutely refused to eat anything green and despite being a cartoonist he couldn't tell a joke to save himself." Her eyes lifted, sheened with tears. "But he was perfect for me. We were perfect for each other, since he ignored my flaws, too. To get cheated out of not even being able to raise his child..." She looked away.

Kevin studied her profile for a moment, then said, "And when he died, it was like he took the light with him, right?"

Her eyes shot to his. "I don't know that I actually ever thought of it that way, but...yes. That's exactly how it feels. How on earth did you—?"

"Chalk it up to way too many hungover mornings watching way too many really sappy talk shows."

She grabbed another hunk of paper, jerkily folded it around the platter. "We need to wrap this all back up."

"No, we don't," Kevin said, pulling the half-smothered plate out of her hands and tossing the crumpled paper aside. "We need—*you* need—to get this out in the open. No, listen to me—"

"Why? So you can toss more glib comments in my direction?" She looked at him, hurt, then grabbed the plate from him again. "If it's all the same to you, I'd really appreciate not having my life reduced to an episode of *Oprah.*"

"I'm not! I was just trying to lighten things up a little, I didn't mean—"

"This isn't a *joke,* Kevin!"

"I know that! And it was a stupid thing to say, even if I didn't mean anything by it. But, be honest...do you really think Gil would want this?"

Once again her gaze swung to his, that neat little crease carved between her brows. "Want what?"

"You keeping all this stuff packed up where nobody can see it. After all the trouble he went to, nagging you to make up those samples, sellin' 'em for ya...if it was me, frankly I'd be pissed as hell. I'd be sitting up there in heaven, thinking, *God, what a waste.* And about more than your work. Because it's like you're keeping *yourself* all tucked away out of sight, too."

Her head whipped around. "You just won't quit about this, will you?"

For a moment Kevin watched her back expand, contract with her short, sharp breaths, then he skootched up behind her to snag her chin with his fingers, forcing her to face him. "Damn straight I'm not quitting about this. Because the new-and-improved Kevin Vaccaro doesn't give up on people. Got it?"

Despite the apprehension radiating from her, she didn't move. Or, amazingly, speak. His own heart hammering in his chest, Kevin smoothed away a strand of hair dangling alongside her cheek. "Maybe you think you're keepin' your heart all locked up and safe," he said, "but I got news for you—it's so big, some of it keeps leaking out, anyway. So big, in fact, that you'd put a stranger's right to know that he had a daughter ahead of your own feelings." He felt his throat work. "You're one in a million, Julie, you know that?"

Several beats passed before she pushed herself to her feet, then slowly walked over to the shelves holding the other boxes. Kevin stood, as well, thumbs tucked in his jeans' waistband, steeling himself for the fallout. But instead she said, "That must've been some talk show."

"Nah, that all came from right in here," Kevin said, waiting for her to turn before he tapped his head. "Honey…Gil didn't take the light with him. He couldn't. Because you're the source, see? You always were."

"Don't—"

"What? Tell you the truth, at least like I see it? When I saw you feeding Pip, and I said it was like the light was comin' from someplace inside you? That's what I'm talking about. Maybe…maybe Gil made you want to turn it on again, but you're the only one with access to the switch."

Long seconds passed until, at last, Julianne closed the space between them. "I don't think that came from your head at all," she said, lifting troubled, confused eyes to his…followed by her palm gently pressing his chest, sending startled flickers of sensation across his skin. "I think it came from right…here."

Kevin covered her hand with his, then drew her close. After *maybe* a moment of resistance, she melted into his arms. Not completely, perhaps, but enough. For now. If things never went beyond this point, he'd be okay with that.

Really.

"One question," he murmured into her hair.

"Mmm?"

"How can you be mad as hell at me one minute and look like you want me to kiss you the next?"

Her head jerked back. "What makes you think—"

The question ended in a shudder when Kevin palmed her jaw, dragged his thumb across her lower lip. *Soft,* he thought, his own mouth tingling with anticipation. "You want a minute to think about your answer?"

"Yes," she whispered, closing her eyes as their lips met, and Kevin thought, *If Victor walks in right now, I'm dead.*

Chapter Nine

One day, Julianne thought, she'd think back on this moment and wonder what on earth had possessed her to kiss Kevin Vaccaro. Or let him kiss her. Whatever. But all those whys and what-were-you-thinkings were years in the future, eons, practically, so instead she decided to enjoy it for as long as it lasted.

And oh, my, was there a lot to enjoy.

If the transpiring of events had startled him, he didn't let on. In fact, she was pretty sure a grin flashed across his mouth an instant before touchdown, even though she was equally sure—if not more so—that he hadn't said all that simply to manipulate the moment. Not Kevin, who was—

His free hand cradled the back of her head as his mouth—warm, firm, insistent—moved over hers, before shifting to place little kisses at the corners of her lips, her cheeks, *that* spot behind her ear.

—completely guileless.

Incredibly good at this, but guileless.

Stupid, Julianne thought, in sync with his heartbeat, so strong and sure underneath her hand. *Wrong. Pointless. Crazy.* She remembered Gil, felt the hot spurt of guilt.

Then Kevin shifted to take her face full in his hands, the kiss this time careful and hot and sweet and tender and wonderful, and she thought, *Alive.*

Here.

Now.

Come back, she called out, if feebly, to Reason and Logic and Self-Preservation, as she felt the heat of Kevin's hands on her ribs, through her dress, and that, too, was wonderful. Still wrong, still pointless, still definitely crazy, but wonderful all the same.

It had been far too long since she'd had *wonderful* in her life.

"You're toying with me," Kevin said, breaking the spell just enough for Reason, Logic and Self-Preservation to come wearily trooping back, settling inside her head with long-suffering sighs. *Be grateful,* she thought. *You don't really want this.*

"Do you mind?" she said. Not letting go of him. Wondering what would happen if her father were to walk in on them right now.

"Not at all," he said, but not before she saw the flash of disappointment. "However…" He set her apart, bending slightly to look into her eyes. "My guess is you don't really want where this is headed."

Oh, dear God…

"And isn't somebody sure of himself this morning?"

One corner of his mouth tucked up. "Julianne…we were just talking about your husband. It's pretty obvious you still miss him. That you miss…what you had with him. My guess is that it probably wouldn't have mattered who was sitting there at that moment, as long as he had the right equipment."

For a moment she was tempted to take umbrage, until she realized he wasn't being rude, he was just trying to save his butt.

Now she felt a helluva lot more than a spurt of guilt. Try a deluge.

Warmth surged up her neck, that she could be so thoughtless. So selfish, acting on an impetuous, hormone-riddled impulse driven by, yes, loneliness and need and the kind words of an unselfish man, without taking two seconds to consider his feelings. Even so…

"You're right. And you're wrong," she said, Reason, Logic and Self-Preservation—now recovered, thank you—shooing away the hormones until she could barely hear their squawks and clucks. "Maybe I did get carried away—" a cluck or two sounded in the distance "—but I'm not indiscriminate. Or desperate. Believe me, I would not have kissed just 'anybody.'"

Kevin grinned. "Yeah?" he said, and Julianne thought, *One day, chickie, you're going to learn to lie.* "So how come you kissed me?"

"Again, with the questions," she said lightly, one eye on those hormones over yonder, doing the Funky Chicken in time to her pounding heart. Then she turned smartly to face the box yawning open at her feet. When she stooped to pick it up, she caught Kevin looking at her, one eyebrow lifted.

"Not a word," she said, hefting it into her arms and heading out of the garage.

Victor was still in the kitchen when they returned, doing—or so it seemed to Kevin—a really bad job of playing cool and collected.

"I was about to send out the dog," he said, which prompted Gus, splayed on his back in a splotch of sun, one paw outstretched, to open one eye and wag his tail. Once. Then Victor apparently noticed his daughter's arms full of box, and Kevin gave silent, fervent thanks for a reason for their delayed return. "Julie…?"

She thunked the box up onto the counter, then dug inside it. "I'd forgotten all about this stuff," she said matter-of-factly, unwrapping the spoon rest and laying it on the stovetop. "So I brought it back out. It'll look good once the cabinets are done, don't you think?" The monitor on the counter emitted a tiny, pissed-baby squawk. "My gracious, is it that late already?" she said, and scooted out of the kitchen.

With more color in her cheeks than Victor's roses.

Kevin carried a cabinet door outside, to a pair of sawhorses already set up on the patio. Naturally, Victor followed him, on the pretense of inspecting the very rambling rose Kevin had just thought of, running riot up one of the corner supports.

"You have no idea how much it's killing me not to ask what happened," Julianne's dad said, picking up a pair of clippers to trim the dead blooms. "Not that I imagine you'd tell me, anyway."

"Nope," Kevin said mildly, setting the cabinet door across the horses. "Except..." He met Victor's practically quivering gaze. "Don't look now, but I'm guessing Julianne's starting to float right side up again, at least a lot more than she useta."

Not surprisingly, Victor didn't look particularly comforted.

Julianne had been dead wrong about one thing: the folly of her lip-lock with Kevin not only didn't wait for years to whap her upside the head, it apparently couldn't even wait out the day. She thought of Robyn, flitting from relationship to relationship, and wondered, *How did you do it?* a moment before she felt a searing rush of shame that should have more than canceled out the various and sundry other hot rushes she'd experienced in the past few hours.

But alas, no.

Dad and Kevin had gone to Home Depot, leaving her with Pip, down for her afternoon nap. The baby had also finally begun to sleep for longer stretches at night, thank God. Julianne had only heard her awaken once, somewhere around five, but as usual Kevin had gotten to the baby before she had.

Standing in the middle of the living room, tears welled in her eyes: could she be any more useless? Kevin was too much of a gentleman—or too smart—to come right out and say that, but that was the real message behind all the big-heart-and-light-from-within stuff, wasn't it? Not that she hadn't served a viable purpose over the past year or so, taking care of her father and Robyn and Pip. But channeling all her energies into other people's lives to the neglect of her own?

Or rather, as an excuse to *ignore* her own?

There was so much wrong with that picture she didn't even know where to begin.

She'd wandered over to the French doors leading out back, Kevin's words lodged in her brain. Especially the part about how it was up to her to flip the switch back on.

Her. Not anyone else.

Her gaze drifted to the pottery studio, and for the first time in forever she actually felt something like a tingle in her fingers, an itch to sink them into a wedge of cool, smooth clay....

The doorbell's chime jarred her out of dreamland. As she crossed to the door, she caught sight through the picture window of an unfamiliar sedan parked in front. She checked the peep hole. At the glimpse of the tall, attractive woman on the other side, Julianne let out a soft gasp.

"Beth!" she said, swinging the door open. A second later her father's old girlfriend had engulfed her in a hug. "What on earth—"

"I was at the Sheltons' party the other night. Didn't he tell you?"

Something in the older woman's eyes kept the "Uh-uh" from escaping Julianne's lips. "Oh, of course, I just spaced out for a second—"

"Oh, sweetie...you're a terrible liar."

Julianne smirked. "I'm also a terrible hostess. Come in,

please," she said, stepping aside. "Dad's not here at the moment, but he shouldn't be long. I was just about to get the baby up."

"The baby…? Oh, Pippa! Oh, my goodness—do you mind if I come with you? Your father couldn't stop talking about what a cutie she is!"

"No, no, of course not," Julianne said, smiling over the *Did I miss something?* clanging inside her head. She'd only met Beth once, at Thanksgiving several years ago, but they'd hit if off immediately. Julianne remembered thinking at the time how perfect Beth would have been for her father. While she'd understood Dad's reasons for not pursuing the relationship, she'd also always wondered, not if, but how much he'd regretted letting her get away.

So what the heck was going on now?

"How are you doing?" Beth asked from behind Julianne as they climbed the stairs.

That was the sixty-four-thousand-dollar question, wasn't it? "Coping," she decided to say. "It's kind of been one thing after another."

"Yes. I gathered." When they reached the second-floor landing, Beth laid a hand on Julianne's arm, her eyes swimming with sympathy. "I was so sorry to hear about your sister. And Gil. I know words are meaningless, but I also know how hard it is, losing someone you loved."

Julianne always hated these moments, never quite knowing what to say or exactly the right proportion of sadness to fortitude. Now she settled on a simple, heartfelt, "Thank you." As they approached the baby's room, she said, "How much did Dad tell you about what's going on with Pip?"

She heard the slight hesitation before Beth said, "You mean, that her father showed up out of the blue and is now living with you?"

The baby was already wide-awake when they went into her room, chatting to her mobile. At the sound of voices, though, she flipped onto her tummy and gave Julianne a huge, gummy grin.

"Yes," Julianne said as Beth exclaimed, "Oh, my goodness—Victor was not exaggerating! What an absolutely adorable baby!" She turned to Julianne, eyes alight. "Do you think she'd let me change her?"

Julianne smiled at Beth, who was one of those women who could somehow pull off elegant in a feedbag. Or, in this case, a striped tunic and red capris. She wore just enough makeup to look good but not desperate, just enough perfume to be distinctive but not overpowering, and was, in Julianne's opinion, the poster child for Age Is Just a Number.

"Sure thing. Knock yourself out."

Gnawing on her own hand, Pip frowned slightly when Beth lifted her out of her crib, only to immediately return the woman's bright, infectious smile.

"I'm a grandmother three times over," she said, carrying Pip to her changing table, "but my son only had boys. And had no interest in trying again for a girl," she added with a light laugh as she laid the baby down. "Three times—four, counting when I was pregnant with my son—I walked through the little girls' department in the stores, hoping. But, nope. Wasn't meant to be." She laughed, getting a Pippa chuckle in response. "Not that the boys aren't completely dear, but there is something very, very special about a little girl...."

"Beth, I'm sorry...but why are you here?"

A brief, shuttered glance preceded a soft, "Would you be offended if I said that's between your father and me?"

"No," Julianne said, flushing. "Absolutely, you're right. It's none of my business. But he wasn't expecting you, was he?"

Her eyes fixed on the baby as she changed her, Beth shook her head. "No," she said, even more softly. The fresh diaper taped, she snapped up the baby's Onesie. "I think this is called 'Going for broke.'" She turned, Pippa securely in her arms. "Now. What's next? A bottle?"

"Just juice, yes. She gets dinner at five."

"Marvelous. Lead the way."

Once in the living room, settled on the sofa facing the doorway with Pip noisily chugging her apple juice, Beth looked over at Julianne. "So tell me about this Kevin."

At the mention of his name, Julianne felt her face warm again. Beth's blond, unplucked brows rose. "Oh, dear. Apparently there's more to tell than I'd thought. I only meant—"

"I know what you meant," Julianne said, sitting stiffly on the edge of the other sofa. "It's just warm in here." Gus lumbered into the room, sniffed Beth's knees, slurped Pip's bare foot, then collapsed with a groan at Beth's feet. "I imagine Dad filled you in on his background?"

"That he's a recovering alcoholic, you mean? Yes. He didn't really say much more than that, though." Beth smiled down at the baby, then looked at Julianne again. "Is he good with his daughter?"

"He's wonderful," Julianne admitted, her eyes glued to the baby. "He's…"

"What, sweetie?"

Julianne's own mother had been nothing like Beth, fragile where Beth was indomitable, mercurial where Beth was steady as the proverbial rock. Now, as the woman's genuine affection and concern flowed around her, Julianne felt a pang of regret that, had things worked out differently, perhaps Beth might have been the mother to Robyn she'd so sorely missed.

Or even, Julianne thought selfishly, the mother *she'd* so sorely missed.

But she could only meet Beth's patient, questioning gaze with a shrug. "There's a lot more to him than you'd expect."

"In what way?"

"He's…thoughtful," she said after a moment. "And by that I don't mean in the way you usually use the word, although he's that, too. But he thinks about things more than any man I've ever met."

"More than your father?" Beth asked, one side of her mouth lifted.

Julianne smiled. "Maybe I wouldn't go that far. But pretty darn close. I guess you'd say Kevin's sort of an everyman philosopher. Of course, I've only known him a few weeks, but..." She felt her forehead pinch. "I really like him."

Beth wriggled back farther into the sofa to cross her legs. "And is that a good thing or not?"

"It is what it is," Julianne said simply.

The other woman looked at her for several moments before lowering her gaze again to the baby. "I grieved for my husband so hard and for so long I made myself ill." Her eyes lifted to Julianne's. "I'd had my little romances before I met Jim, of course, but he was the first man to take my breath away. And still did, with amazing regularity, up to the day he died. I couldn't even *fathom* falling in love again. And yet, somehow, inexplicably, I did."

Feeling her pulse beating frantically at the base of her throat, Julianne said, "My father?"

"Yes. Your father." Shaking her head and snuffling a little laugh, Beth glanced toward the window, then back at Julianne. She had the gentlest, and yet the most direct, brown eyes. Eyes that laid whatever the woman was thinking and feeling right out there for God and everybody to see.

"After Jim died, I wrapped what was familiar and safe around me as tightly as a swaddled newborn. I couldn't bear to think about selling our house—it would have been like losing Jim all over again. Then I met Victor. And ironically, he was the one who convinced me that starting a new chapter of my own life meant no disrespect to my dead husband. Of course," she said with a light laugh, "at the time he was talking about downsizing from a four-bedroom house to a condo. Not about falling in love a second time."

Julianne's eyes dropped to her hands, folded on her lap, as Beth's words winnowed inside her, squeezing her heart like a boa constrictor.

"It's absolutely terrifying," Beth said quietly, "opening yourself up to that again. The possibility of more hurt, more heartbreak. But what's the alternative?"

The sudden sound of voices coming from the kitchen cut off whatever else Beth had been about to say. "There they are," Julianne said, practically springing from the chair. But before she got halfway across the room, her father popped through the archway between the living and dining rooms. "Julie? Do you know about the car parked in front of the house…?"

He stopped dead in his tracks.

"Beth? What…? I thought you'd left!"

"I changed my mind," she said, sitting the baby upright on her lap to burp her. "Have a seat, Victor. We need to talk."

Julianne took that as her cue to vamoose.

Well, this is a fine mess we've gotten ourselves into, Victor thought as he glanced from one tense face to the other at his dining room table. Except for Beth, that is. In fact, Beth seemed perfectly at ease with not only having virtually invited herself to dinner, but then—after a whirlwind grocery shopping expedition—commandeering his kitchen, spinning magic out of thin air. With a little help from Whole Foods. Damn woman always could cook like nobody's business, he thought grumpily, jabbing a chunk of perfectly seasoned, tender-crunchy asparagus into his mouth.

And damn her for…for being *her.* For having the gall to not give up on him.

On them.

Turning her down the first time had nearly killed him. So on a scale of one to ten, he figured his chances of living through a second round were about a minus five.

How dare she show up in his own living room, throwing his own words back in his face, demanding—not pleading, not begging, *demanding!*—that he rethink a thing or two, about how sacrificing yourself for the good of someone else rarely works. That, yes, there wasn't a better father in the world, but maybe now it was time he live his own life. And that, if he wasn't getting the message, she could recommend this terrific book by this guy named Victor Booth, perhaps he'd heard of him?

"This is really, really great," Kevin said, grinning around a mouthful of pasta, and Victor glowered, thinking, even more grumpily, *And then there's you.*

Dammit, the kid wasn't supposed to grow on him. Wasn't supposed to turn out to be decent. Honorable. Dependable. Not to mention the first person to finally jar Julianne out of her stupor.

To, perhaps, jar Victor out of his.

"Thank you!" Beth said, beaming, warm and generous and beautiful, a sixty-one-year-old siren in sporty casual or whatever the hell it was called, and Victor closed his eyes to keep his brain from exploding.

"Dad? Are you okay?"

Julie. Worried. Not eating again. Hand knotted by her plate, anxiety tightening her mouth.

Kevin. Handsome. Solid. Watching Julie, concern pulsing from every fiber of his not inconsiderable being.

Beth. Gaze bouncing from Julie to Kevin to Victor, a small, irritatingly knowing smile playing across her mouth.

"I'm fine, honey," Victor finally said, stuffing the last bite of roll in his mouth.

You can't protect her forever, Beth had said—both then, about Robyn, and now, about Julie. And now, as then, his gut churned with the truth of it. The frustration. Only, *then* he'd still thought... *Maybe.* Now the light was finally beginning to dawn that there was only so much he could do.

Maybe he should go read that book.

"Dessert?" Beth said, smiling, rising from the table. Giving Victor's shoulder a little squeeze as she passed him on her way back to the kitchen.

While he and Kevin had been out, Kevin had mentioned the job possibility back East, although he'd been quick to reassure Victor that he sincerely doubted anything would come of it. Not quick enough, however, that Victor hadn't seen the hunger in the young man's eyes. The yearning.

If it happens, go for it, he'd wanted to say. Even though he knew what that would mean, that Kevin would take Victor's only grandchild more than two thousand miles away. That Julianne—making noises about how *wonderful* dessert looked—would be heartbroken.

Life would be so much easier if it came with warning labels, Victor thought, morosely digging into the best tiramisu he'd ever eaten in his life.

"And wouldn't that be a kick in the ass," Felix mused to Kevin as they walked out to their trucks after an AA meeting, several days after Beth's surprise visit, "if Victor actually took the woman up on her offer?"

"A total shock, is what it would be," Kevin said, carefully unlocking his door, the handle still hot after the ninety-five-degree day. Brother. Had that been a weird night or what? Not that he hadn't liked Beth—what was not to like, the woman was great—but it was pretty obvious she'd given Victor some sort of an ultimatum about reconsidering moving back East to be with her.

"Thought you said he had it bad for the woman?"

"He does. At least, from what I can tell. But fat chance of him leaving Julianne and Pip. Or that house."

"I thought you liked the house?"

"I do like the house. Which looks a helluva lot better without those godawful yellow cabinets, by the way. But it's just a freaking *house,* y'know? Yeah, his parents built it and everything, but... Sorry, if it was me, and somebody like that came along, I'd ditch the damn house so fast it wouldn't even be funny."

Felix eyed him for a moment before, on a shrug, he opened his own truck door. "Who knew you were such a romantic, eh?"

"It's got nothing to do with romance, it's about bein' practical. About...about not hanging on to something that isn't working for you anymore."

Felix cocked his head. "We still talking about the house?"

Kevin blew a stiff breath through his nose. Because Victor, who'd left that morning for his conference, wasn't the only one walking around like the earth might momentarily open up at his feet. For days Julianne had been bouncing back and forth between funny and friendly, and quiet and withdrawn. Frankly, it was about to drive him right over the edge.

"No," he gritted out, "we're not talking about the house."

Felix laughed. "I know that look. That, my frien', is the look of a man in loooove." He drew out the word, cackling evilly—and ducking—when Kevin took a halfhearted swing at his shoulder.

"It's the look of a man smart enough to know futility when it's starin' him in the face," Kevin said. Felix didn't know about the kiss. Nobody did. Not even his brother Rudy, whom Kevin talked to almost every day. The way he figured it, see, not talking about it made it less real. Not that it could be much less real—as in, meaningful—than it was, but the last thing he needed was for other people to make *more* of it than it was.

Besides, it was just a kiss. On a guy scale, a kiss barely even rated as significant, right?

Now he looked over at Felix, who was giving him a "heh-heh" look, and sighed. "Okay, so I got feelings for her. But that's it. Nothing's ever gonna come of it, so can we just drop it?"

"Whatever you say," Felix said. Grinning. "So how's it going on the job front?"

He would bring that up. "Okay, I guess. I'm supposed to start Monday with this contractor." Kevin waited out the stupid pang of disappointment that, as he'd expected, the guy back east had never called. Not that he could have taken the job, anyway, but still. It would've been cool to be asked.

Man, was life teasing him with a bunch of stuff he couldn't have, or what?

As if reading his mind, Felix suddenly said, "You know... sometimes I think we settle a lot more than we really have to. Because maybe we don' think we deserve better, you know? Or that life's pushed us into a corner an' there's no way out. You're thinking, hey—no way in hell am I good enough for this woman, so you tell yourself there's no chance. You don' even try. When maybe she's thinking the same thing."

Kevin laughed out loud. "Trust me, she's not thinking the same thing. What she's thinking is that nobody can compare with what she had. Not me, not anybody. And maybe I'm not in the mood to compete with a ghost."

"So what's this ghost gonna do, huh? Come back from the grave and beat you up? So, what? You jus' gonna walk away?"

He glared at his friend. "She already said no, Felix."

"No to you? Or no in general?"

"Does it matter?"

"Does it matter? Does it *matter?*" His friend was booming by this time, attracting the notice of other people in the parking lot. "Are you *loco?* You bet your sweet ass it matters!" Then, grumbling, he batted in Kevin's general direction before climbing into his truck. "An' why am I wasting my time, talkin' to the air?" His engine growled to life. A second later the old man leaned out his open window and bellowed, "Hey. You been to that eBay recently?"

"No. Why?"

"I hear you can buy jus' about anything there. You should check it out, see if maybe somebody's tryin' to sell some *cojones!*"

Then, cackling, he gunned his truck out of the parking space and roared into the night.

Fifteen minutes later, his head spinning, Kevin pulled into Victor's driveway. Except for a light in Julie's room, the house was dark. And eerily silent, he realized when he walked through the front door, except for the soothing whoosh of the swamp cooler. And Gus, who woofed his version of a joyful greeting, then disappeared, only to return a moment later, his food dish clamped between his teeth, a hopeful look in his little yellow eyes.

Chuckling, Kevin pocketed his keys and followed the dog to the kitchen to, first, fill the bowl with kibble, then forage for himself, thinking—with a not-little pinch of regret—that it was gonna be a bitch, having to keep his own kitchen stocked one day soon. Which reminded him, he really needed to start thinking about cranking up the apartment search again. Although, come to think of it, he might as well wait until after his sister's wedding, right?

Oddly buoyed by this thought—like finding out your dental appointment's been pushed back another week—Kevin plodded out to the living room, a ham-and-cheese sandwich clamped in one hand, a glass of milk in the other, the dog panting along behind. Hands full, he shouldered the wall switch to turn on the lamps on either side of the sofa.

Boxes. Everywhere. On the coffee table, the chairs, the sofa, stacked two and three deep on the floor. Some still taped shut; some open, some—judging from the winged, costumed critters and piles of crumpled newsprint crowded into whatever space wasn't taken up by the boxes—apparently empty.

"I made a decision," Julianne said behind him.

"You made a mess, is what you made," Kevin said. She laughed. He turned, chewing, saw her with Pip slumped in her arms, cute little mouth sagging open as she sawed logs, and thought, *Yes, please.*

"I've been on the phone all day," Julianne said, her glasses crooked, doing that instinctive swaying thing with the baby. Her hair looked like she'd let Pip practice her hairstyling techniques on it; a tattered cobweb or two clung to her clothes. Kevin wanted to kiss her so badly he couldn't stand it. "Calling gallery owners, sending them photos… God, how did we survive before picture phones?"

"It boggles the mind." Kevin stuffed the last of his sandwich in his mouth and mumbled, "So what happened?" around it.

Julianne grinned, looking so pleased with herself it made Kevin's eyes sting. "I have six appointments tomorrow. Three here, three in Santa Fe."

"Get out."

"It's true," she said with one of those ohmigod-what-have-I-done? giggles. "Because you were right," she said on a little sigh. "Gil would have a cow if he thought all his nagging had been for naught. I at least owe him this much."

Kevin took a sip of his milk. "You owe it to yourself, Julie."

"I know." She swallowed, then repeated very softly, "I know."

His glass of milk set on the corner of an end table, Kevin extended one arm. "Come here," he said, and she did, and he wrapped that arm around both her and the baby and said, "Didn't I tell ya you had a hot item there?"

"Don't get too excited," she said, leaning into him, smelling of dust and shampoo and baby. "They're not sold yet. We're only talking appointments to show samples to gallery owners."

"And I guarantee you, if sucky phone pics got you six appointments, the real thing's gonna knock their socks off." He took the baby from her, grunting when Pip slumped against his collarbone without so much as a whimper. "Geez…what'd you feed this kid?" he whispered, brushing his lips over his daughter's fluffy hair, his daughter's scent mixed with Julianne's giving him a head rush. "Rocks?"

When he looked over at Julianne, however, the look on her face nearly broke his heart. Was she imagining what it might have been like, if it'd been Gil instead of him, holding their own baby? But as bad as he felt for her, he refused to go down that path. Or to let her. "So," Kevin said, determined to get everybody back on track, "did you tell your dad?"

"What? Oh. No. Not yet. If something comes of it—"

"*When* something comes of it."

"Okay, *when* something comes of it," she said, smiling, stroking Pip's back, "I'd rather it be a done deal."

"So he can't try to talk you out of it?"

"I don't know that he'd try to talk me out of it, but he'd definitely fuss." She sighed. "I know Dad can be a bit of a worrywart, but…can you blame him?"

"No," Kevin said, palming his daughter's head, the sweet-hot surge of protectiveness that shot through him nearly knocking him over. "Not at all." Then he lifted his gaze to her aunt and felt another, entirely different type of surge, just as sweet but much, *much* hotter.

Then suddenly Julianne's nose wrinkled. Was that cute or what? "But I was just wondering…if maybe you'd like to come with me? I mean, if you're not busy. And not because I need anybody to hold my hand or anything…I'd just, well—" more wrinkling "—like your company?"

Well, hell, Kevin thought, as the surges damn near caused a meltdown. And if he had any sense, he'd simply say, "Sure, that'd be great," walk right past the sleeping rattlesnake without poking it to see if it was alive. But no, he had to go and ask, "As your friend?"

For, like, five million seconds, Julianne stared at him. Not like she was shocked or mad or even surprised, but with one of those "Yeah, I figured you'd ask that" expressions. Then she released the longest sigh he'd ever heard come out of another human being's mouth.

"And wouldn't it be convenient if we got together because of Pip?"

Kevin felt like he'd been run over by a freight train. "You think I'm cozying up to you because of the baby?"

"The thought had occurred to me."

"Well, you can just knock that idea right outta your head, because what I feel for you has nothing to do with Pip."

Her head cocked. "What you feel for me?"

Aw, hell. "Yeah. What I feel for you. And don't get all hot and bothered, because I don't know myself what that is, exactly, except that it's good. Or maybe not good, depending on your point of view. But it's real. And it's got nothing to do with Pip. Whatever I am, or have been, I'm not a player. You got that?"

That got a shaky smile before Julianne walked over to pick up a platter, circled with longhorn steers in cowboy boots. "Being around you…I really do feel a little like Sleeping Beauty, coming out of my coma. But…"

"Yeah, I know. Only one Prince Charming to a customer."

Tears glittered in her eyes. "Please don't be angry, Kevin, I can't help how I feel. No, I'm not done. Since I met you, I definitely feel…calmer. More hopeful. That I might actually be whole again someday. But I have no idea what that means, either. What you said, about me being the only one who can flip that switch to turn the light back on inside me? It makes perfect sense. But nobody can force me to do it before I'm ready."

And while he couldn't exactly take that as encouragement, still—*before I'm ready* was light-years ahead of *fuggedaboutit*. Hope and fear tangling inside his head, Kevin crossed to Julianne and gathered her to his side, kissing her rumpled, dusty hair. "It's okay, honey," he whispered. "We have all the time in the world."

"Good," she said, obviously relieved. "Then let's put this little girl to bed, so you can help me decide which pieces I should take on these appointments tomorrow."

Not exactly an invitation to get naked together, but as first steps went, it'd do. It'd do just fine.

Chapter Ten

"I don't think I told you," Beth said as she and Victor strolled barefoot along the moonlit beach, hand in hand, "but I recently inherited a little waterfront house in South Carolina, from one of my aunts. So if you moved back east with me, we could do this more often."

"What? Get sand between our toes? Dodge hurricanes?"

"Wimp," she said, her filmy scarf plastering itself to Victor's chest in the salty breeze.

"So sue me for preferring to live someplace where I don't have to worry about my house blowing down."

Beth laughed. "You're impossible."

"And you're pushing."

Leaning into him, she squeezed his hand. "So sue me," she said gently, "for taking your invitation to tag along to a conference in Maui as encouragement." Swiping a strand of hair out of her face, she lifted her face toward the gleaming breakers lapping at the shore, the full moon rising ever higher from its hula-ing twin in the shimmering water. "Was I wrong?"

"No." Victor let go of her hand to sling one arm around her shoulder, cool and bare and smooth over a strapless top. "I had to see—"

"How you felt?"

"No, I know how I feel," he said, kissing her temple. "What I can *do* about it. However..." He sighed. Beth lightly rubbed his stomach, igniting a flame he'd thought long since doused for good.

"Julianne doesn't know I'm here, does she?"

"I thought it best not to...involve her."

Beth peered up at him, frowning slightly. "Worry her, you mean." When he started to protest, she cut him off with, "It's okay, Jim was the same way about Matt. He was far more of a Nervous Nelly about our son than I was." On a soft laugh, she said, "Damn man couldn't sleep for weeks after the kid left for college."

"Must have driven you nuts."

"You have no idea. And yet, somehow I loved him even more for it."

"But...?" She shrugged. Victor grimaced. "I just can't leave Julie high and dry, Beth. How can I think about my own needs when she's still so fragile?" After several seconds of listening to the waves' relentless sucking at the shore, he said, "Okay—what aren't you saying?"

"You know damn well what I'm not saying."

"You're angry."

"I'm not angry, I'm...confused. Why *did* you bring me here if it wasn't going to make any difference?"

"Beth, I swear I didn't get on that plane with my mind already made up—"

"Oh, for heaven's sake, Victor! In all the years I've known you, you've *never* put yourself at the top of your to-do list. First with Robyn, now with Julianne. And it's not that I don't admire you for it—frankly, it's probably one of the reasons I love *you* so much—but the situations aren't even remotely the same. Julianne's getting over a huge blow, I know, and my heart aches for her. Because I've been there. As have you," she quietly added. "But she *is* getting over it. And unlike her sister, she's not in any danger of self-destructing, not from what I could tell." She took a deep breath. "Victor, I know how this is going to sound…but coddling Julianne won't make up for losing Robyn."

He came to a dead stop. "Is that what you think I'm doing?"

"I know that's what you're doing!" Beth said, her gaze imploring. "But you can't stop her from taking her own chances, maybe even falling in love, no matter how much it scares you."

"Falling in— You think she's falling in love with *Kevin?* No, no…that's impossible—she'd never do that."

"Why? Because you don't want her to? Because you don't want her to suffer again? Well, here's a news flash, sweetie—you don't get a say in this. You not only don't have the right to protect her from this, you can't."

Poleaxed, Victor stared dumbly at Beth. "You're really sure that's what's happening?"

"Sure? No. Frankly, my guess is Julie hasn't even admitted it to herself yet. But I do have two eyes in my head. And she's got all the signs. However…"

Wrapping long, strong arms around his waist, Beth looked up at Victor, her expression resigned. "*I* have no right to interfere, either. After all, I left everything I'd known to be closer to my Matt and his family. So I can't exactly fault you for wanting to stick close by your daughter, to watch out for her, can I?"

Victor's eyes narrowed. "Why the about-face? A second ago—"

"—I said my piece. And I meant it. But I also know you are who you are, and you're going to do whatever you think is best. And whatever that is—" she shrugged "—I'm fine with it."

"Really?"

"What choice do I have? Now how about we go back to our room and make the most of whatever time we have together?"

Victor kissed her, long and slow and deep, then slipped her hands from around his waist to link their fingers, leading her back to the hotel. "You're one remarkable woman, Bethany Forrest."

"Took you long enough to figure that out," she said, leaning into him as they walked.

"And as I said originally," Julianne said, extending her hand to the last of the six gallery owners on her list, "I do have other offers. So I'll get back to you with my decision in a couple of days."

Crouched unobtrusively in an out-of-the-way corner as he repacked the samples, Kevin hid his smile. Especially when the woman, weighed down with silver jewelry, seemed to have trouble finding her voice. "But we have the perfect clientele for your work—"

"Oh, absolutely! I just need time to think about it. Especially since your commission is a bit higher than standard."

Three-inch-long liquid silver earrings shimmered like waterfalls when the woman's chin jutted out. "Which would be more than offset by our traffic."

Julianne smiled. "And since I can only work so fast, I have to take the time/profit ratio into consideration. So. As I said, I'll get back to you soon, I promise." After another glance around the colorful gallery, she added, "I can see why your customers are so loyal—you have incredible taste!"

Kevin nearly choked. Six galleries they'd visited. Six times Julie had closed her pitch with almost the same line. What an eye-opener, watching her in hard-nosed-salesperson mode—an entirely new persona, she swore, since Gil had been her front man the first time around. But all afternoon, dressed in a deep-pink sundress and high-heeled sandals that said—according to her—creative, but not flaky, she hadn't shown a single sign of the nervousness that had kept her in the bathroom so long this morning Kevin had begun to wonder if they'd ever get out of the house.

Now, back in the Camry, everything stowed safely in the trunk, she seemed to melt into her seat. But with a very smug grin on her face. Kevin squeezed her hand, then pulled out of the parking lot. Her handing him the car keys had been a testament in itself as to how tired she was.

"It's over, honey. Ya done good."

"I guess it didn't go too badly, huh?"

"Are you kiddin'? You were hell on heels."

She burst out laughing, then turned to him, eyes glittering. She swore she didn't wear tinted contacts, but her eyes sure looked a lot brighter blue than usual. "Did you see how many people were ogling the stuff during my last pitch?"

"I did. Somehow, I doubt they'd have any trouble moving it."

"I agree," she said dreamily. Kevin chuckled softly.

"You little monkey. You've already made up your mind, haven't you?"

"More or less. That place out on Canyon Road in Santa Fe, and then the one we just left. Both want exclusives, but since it's two different cities—" Her cell rang. "Yes? Oh, hi, Ms. Martinez..." She turned to Kevin, brows raised. "I see.... Yes, that would definitely make a difference, I'll certainly keep that in mind.... Yes, I promise, the day after tomorrow at the very latest. And thanks so much for calling... Absolutely, I think your gallery would showcase my work wonderfully, too. Bye."

She clapped shut her phone, holding it close to her chest.

"I take it we have a done deal?"

"She said she'd lower her commission if I gave her the Albuquerque exclusive. And that she wanted to showcase the Fairy Tales line all next month."

"*Yes!*" Kevin said, bumping knuckles with her across the gearshift. "So, what next?"

Julianne angled her head. "It's about this baby we need to pick up?"

"I knew that," he said, heading toward Felix's house. They'd both decided that hauling a five-month-old around probably wouldn't have presented the most professional image, so Kevin suggested they leave Pip with Felix's wife, Lupe. To his amazement, Julianne agreed. Even said she completely trusted him.

The question was, he wondered, as they pulled into Felix's driveway underneath a huge, feathery mimosa just coming into peach-scented bloom...how was she defining *completely?*

Thanks to a freeway traffic snarl, they didn't get back to the house until after seven. While Julianne fed a very hungry Pip—who was now scarfing cereal and baby veggies like they were going out of style—Kevin headed back out to, as he put it, hunt down something for dinner. He'd suggested they go out to eat to celebrate, but Julianne was way too pooped to face the whole baby-in-a-restaurant scene. Even if the baby—she spooned a glob of sweet potato puree into the most adorable little mouth in the world—was Pip.

And even though she couldn't remember the last time it had felt so good to be tired. Not to mention so...ballsy.

Had that actually been her, stringing those gallery owners along, making them feel as though she'd be doing *them* a favor by letting them rep her work? Most artists would sell their souls for the chance at putting a few pieces in *one* gallery. And yet, taking the safer route—or the first offer—hadn't even occurred to her. Of course, it probably hadn't hurt that the first owner had pounced like a cat on catnip. Nice little ego boost, that—

"Pip! No!" Julianne cried, her face and chest suddenly flocked with a fine coating of rejected sweet potatoes. So much for that adorable little mouth. Not to mention the ego boost.

"Hey," boomed Kevin, who happened into the kitchen, laden with bulging grocery bags, just in time to witness his daughter's first act of defiance. The baby jumped, her lower lip sucked in, her eyes huge in the classic "Who, me?" expression, and Julianne dissolved into giggles as Kevin wagged his finger at the tiny girl. "Don't play with your food, young lady!"

Pip's reaction was to pucker up and let loose with round two, this time at her father, followed by an enormous, contagious belly laugh that reduced Julianne to helpless, overtired, laughter-into-tears hysterics.

"What the—" Kevin immediately squatted beside her, his expression so concerned she couldn't decide whether to continue crying or start laughing again. "Honey? What's wrong?"

Where would you like me to start? she wanted to say. Because instead of clarifying things, her whole I'm-the-only-one-who-can-flip-the-switch schpiel last night had cracked open her protective shell even more. Not to mention left her so abuzz with whacked hormones she felt like a freaking beehive.

"N-nothing's *wrong,*" she said, wiping her face with the damp cloth she'd intended to use on the baby, who was just chillin' in her seat, happy as a little sweet-potato-stuffed clam. "I just feel like…like a penned animal who's suddenly realized the door to its cage is open."

"Yeah, I can see how a baby spitting…whatever the hell this is," Kevin said, wiping his own face with a napkin, "all over you would lead to that conclusion."

"Ah…no," she said, letting her gaze dock with his, giving in to that which had been building all day, every time she heard Kevin's laugh or caught his smile or got sucked into his pheromone bubble. Which apparently encompassed all of Bernalillo

County and half of Sandoval. "This has nothing to do with the baby." She wiped her eyes. Hiccuped. "This has to do with—" she lifted her fingers to sift through a hank of slightly sweet-potatoed, caramel-brown hair that had fallen over his right eye, finishing softly "—you."

For a long moment Kevin looked afraid to breathe. Then he grabbed her hand and pressed a kiss against her knuckles, his eyes never leaving her face. "I thought you wanted slow."

Julianne stood to clean the baby. "My head still does," she whispered, her back to him. "My body apparently has other ideas."

She felt his heat before his hands landed at her waist, his mouth gentle, importunate, against the nape of her neck, and her libido said, *You called?*

"You sure?" he murmured, his breath dancing across her ear, and she tensed, expectant. Frightened. Hopeful.

"I'm not sure of anything," she said, almost sadly. "Except..." She turned, desperate to find answers in that steady, open gaze. "I have no idea who I am anymore. Who that chick was who acted like she was God's gift with those gallery owners, who the hell the chick is who just propositioned a man. I don't *do* that!"

One side of his mouth tilted. "That was a proposition?"

"You couldn't tell?"

"Well, I'd hoped that's what it was. But I didn't wanna presume. Julie," he whispered, rough fingertips careful on her jaw, while the baby looked on, thankfully oblivious. "Why don't we have dinner, put the baby to bed, then see...what happens."

"I have a better idea. How about we put the baby to bed, put dinner in the fridge and go for it before I chicken out?"

Kevin's brows shot up. Then he laughed. "Whoa. You are serious."

"It's been eighteen months. My father's away. And I need to...remember."

His face clouded. "Gil?"

"No! What it was like..." She took a deep breath "To feel." Then a nervous giggle burst from her lips. "Help me find that switch, Kevin. Please."

"In that case," he said, leaning in, "let's see what I can do...."

All day, Julianne had been surprising him. So by this point, Kevin shouldn't have been shocked by anything she said or did, right?

Wrong.

"You're not serious?" he said, when, after he was sure Pip was asleep—which had taken far longer than usual, natch—he'd finally found her in the pool.

Naked.

She was treading water, the last rays of sunlight sluicing off her breasts. "Is this a problem?" It was nearly the end of June. As in, one of the longest days of the year. And yes, there were lots of trees and the privacy wall, but...

"Nope." He set the baby monitor on a small glass table. "Not a problem at all. Although maybe we should wait until it's a little darker...?"

"Where's your sense of adventure?" she said, splashing him. Laughing. Trying just a little too hard.

Kevin dodged most of the spray, then knelt by the edge of the pool, willing the guilt to buzz off. As long as it was her idea it was okay, right? Then she rose like a dolphin to dive back in, and he realized how clear the water was, and he willed the sun to sink. Fast.

Of course, the rippling, sunset-hued stew of blues and oranges and golds distorted...things. But not nearly as much as you might think. Not so much, for instance, that he couldn't see she was a real blonde.

"I would have pegged you as a bit more...reserved."

Laughing, she glided over, hauling herself up to fold her arms at his feet. Through the trees, he caught a glimpse of the Sandia Mountains flashing coral in front of a pale aqua sky. The viscous, molten light drenched Julianne's wet skin, set fire to her slicked-back hair…glided across her left hand, as bare as the rest of her. Through spiked lashes, her eyes were slightly unfocused.

"And I would have pegged you as being a lot easier to seduce."

Oh, man. Kevin reached out to skim water droplets off a cheek as soft as air. "Yeah, well…controlled substances aren't all I've done without this past year."

"And y-yet, you're still dressed."

"I don't want to take advantage of you."

Her smile dimmed. "If anything, it's the other way around. You…do understand that, don't you?"

Yeah. He did—that *she* was kidding herself into believing this was all about sex, that her feelings had nothing to do with it. Too bad for her, then, that he'd believed her when she'd said she'd never propositioned a man before. That she might as well have a T-shirt made up that said *This* Good Girl Doesn't.

Until tonight.

"Got it," he said, then grinned, determined to keep things as light as she wanted 'em. "Have you actually fooled around in a pool before?"

"Does it matter?" she said, blinking away the flicker of doubt in her eyes.

"Not at all. Unless this is about proving something to me."

"It's not. Believe me. Proving something to myself, maybe. But not you. Now, are you going to sit there all night in your clothes or what?"

And with maturity came great responsibility. Or at least common sense. "And as much as I adore my daughter, giving her a sibling right now isn't part of my game plan. Unfortunately, word has it that chlorine's hell on latex."

One waterlogged eyebrow lifted. "You have condoms?"

"Why do you think I volunteered to do the grocery shopping? Hey!" he said, laughing, when she splashed him again. "What can I tell you, the Vaccaros are an optimistic lot."

"If cautious?"

"I can learn from my mistakes, Julie."

She pushed away from the side of the pool as dusk finally settled over the yard like a big, fat cat, sucking the remaining color from the sky. "It's okay," she said, treading water. "I'm…protected."

In one way, at least, he thought, hearing the caution in *her* voice.

"So, please?" she said, her voice barely louder than the hyper cricket lurking in the rose bushes. "Sometime tonight?"

Kevin stood and quickly stripped, diving into the warm water. He surfaced at the far end of the pool, shaking water out of his eyes a moment before Julianne wrapped herself around him. One hand braced on the pool's edge, Kevin tucked his other arm around her back, nipples grazing nipples, goodies grinding into goodies, the darkness preventing him from fully reading her expression. A moot point, however, since a split second later she kissed him like he had never, ever been kissed before, with a sweet aggression that teetered on desperation.

"Whoa, sweetheart," he said as they ratcheted up to warp speed, "you might want to pace yourself."

"After more than a year and a half? In your dreams, big guy."

With that, she guided him backward onto the curved steps in the shallow end to straddle his thighs, the water sloshing frantically around them as she took him inside her. For a moment anger nearly overtook arousal, that she *was* using him to prove something, as part of her recovery process or whatever. And then he got it, that this was like pulling off the bandage in one quick stroke…her way of moving quickly past the memories of the last time she'd done this.

And with whom.

So he let her call the shots, take the lead, content to skim his fingers up and down her back, nuzzling small, extraordinarily sensitive breasts, pale as milk in the first glimmer of moonlight, while she rode him with an almost mindless fury. Tenderness would come later. She, however, was coming...right...*now*....

Out of consideration to her neighbors, Kevin supposed, she bit her lip to keep from crying out. But he felt her orgasm—oh, boy, did he feel it—to his toes. "Now you," she whispered, still shuddering, gripping his hips with her knees to hold him tightly inside her, her eyes popping open in delighted surprise when she climaxed a second time, moments before he did.

"Holy crap," he breathed when there was finally breath to breathe. Still on his lap, Julianne lay molded against him, pliant, trusting, the still-agitated water gently rocking them. "I take it we found the switch?"

She chuckled against his damp neck, muttering something about his being responsible for her second coming. Then she untangled herself to strike out across the pool, her strokes sure, the moonlight gliding off luminous, water-slick skin. At the far end she stopped, treading water. "Join me?"

"I thought I just did."

"Damn, I opened myself up for that one, didn't I?" Kevin laughed. "Oh, *hell*," she said, sliding underneath the surface. Kevin waded out until the water was deep enough to support him, then struck out to meet her, where they somehow managed to embrace without drowning, and their kisses were slow and lazy and crazy, and all he could think was, *So* this *is what I was waiting for.*

Afterward they swam for a while, not talking, not needing to, like the water was some sort of conduit for their feelings. *And thank God for that,* Kevin thought, since, like your typical American male, he wasn't real good at putting what he felt into words. He could show her, though. And intended to, as many times as she'd let him.

"So tell me," he said after they'd hauled themselves back onto dry land and he was thoroughly enjoying drying her off, "*have* you ever done that before?"

"Made love in a swimming pool, you mean?" She grabbed the towel from him and wrapped it around her breasts, her hair a mass of twisted, dripping snakes around her neck. "No. You?"

"Nope."

"How'd you like it?"

"Ranks right up there with the Sox winning the World Series."

"Well, all right," she said, laughing, and he drew her close and kissed her again, then wrapped her in his arms, looking up at the moon and feeling damned smug that she'd done something with him she'd never done with anybody else. And it occurred to him that this was a woman who'd probably keep surprising him for the rest of his life, a thought that scared the hell out of him—that he was putting *Julianne* and *rest of his life* in the same sentence.

Although, the more he thought about it, the less scary it sounded.

Then she cupped him, murmuring, "Again?"

"Mmm, I think we can work something out. Except this time," Kevin said, hauling her up into his arms and striding toward the house, "we do it my way."

"Oh? And what way is that?"

"You'll see," he said, elbowing the patio door shut behind him.

Curled up in his doggy bed in the kitchen, Gus opened one eye as they passed, groaned and went right back to sleep.

Well, hell. She'd gone and done it now, hadn't she?

Why on earth, Juliet wondered a good hour or so after their wet 'n' wild encounter, had she thought that playing the wanton hussy would turn her into one? If she'd never had sex before without being emotionally involved, what in the name of Helen of Troy had made her think this time would be any different?

"We really should probably do something about d-dinner," she murmured as Kevin pressed yet another in a lovely, long series of kisses somewhere between her belly button and heaven.

But, clearly, heaven could wait as he continued his unhurried exploration of an area thoroughly reconnoitered several times already. So, apparently, could his stomach, since he muttered, "Later," and kept going.

And going. And going. And...oh, yes, that was *very* nice, she thought on something between a sigh and a whimper, as he lifted her legs and nibbled down the inside of first one thigh, then the other. *Yes, just like that....* She lifted her hips, begging, and he obliged, his mouth and tongue a miracle, a torment...and once more the warmth pooled and spread and consumed her, consumed them, as he joined her, filling the emptiness she'd ignored for so long.

Julianne closed her eyes, as if that could possibly stanch the emotions also pooling, swirling, buoying her into that hallowed place so far beyond mere physical sensation it could only be called...bliss.

With my body, I thee worship...

"Look at me...at *me*," Kevin gently demanded between kisses that expertly straddled the fine line between tenderness and passion, clasping her hands over her head. Her eyes dragged open just as he pulled back to look at her, *all* of her, as though he'd never seen her before, and she knew what he was asking, that she stay in the now, stay with him, not slip back into the past.

"I'm here," she murmured, as their gazes mirrored their joining, almost desperate that he understand there really was no other place she wanted to be, other than with him, right now. Oh, no. She'd left the past in the pool, in a stifled cry of both pain and joy that had blown grief literally out of the water.

Only to leave in its place something far less easy to define.

"Good," he said, smiling. Stilling. Giving her the chance to fully absorb…everything. The first two times had been hot, fast, mindless. Insanely good. This time Kevin moved as though he had all the time in the world.

With my body, I thee worship…

Tears crowded the corners of her eyes, symbols of a jumble of emotions she couldn't untangle.

I…

I want…

Like a faint glow in the distance, the words struggled to flicker into something bigger and brighter and far more dangerous than she knew she could handle at the moment. Than she might ever be able to handle, she realized, and she tensed, suddenly frightened, his name half sighed, half sobbed.

"What is it?" he whispered, eyes dark, concerned, and Julianne shook her head, wrapping her legs around him, thinking the least she could do was to be as patient with herself as he was.

After all, they had all the time in the world….

Chapter Eleven

Dude, not my room, Kevin thought when sunlight blasted his retinas through his eyelids the next morning. Then he smiled, remembering whose room it was.

Whose bed he was in.

Still smiling, he rolled over, stretching, reaching…

From across the otherwise empty bed, Gus whined, chin propped on mattress, golden eyes fixed on Kevin.

"Julie?" he called out, yawning, as he pulled himself to a sitting position, finally getting a good look at Julianne's room. Peachy walls, dotted with bits of tape that had probably once held up posters. Frilly lace curtains. White iron headboard. A gazillion unceremoniously dumped pillows in the center of the floor. Handpainted chickens on a funky old dresser. A white wicker rocker by the window, smothered in everything he'd seen her wear for the past two weeks.

A teenager's room, he realized as he yawned again, as doubt began to kick awake his brain cells, one by one. Not that Julie and he weren't good together. Oh, they were *good,* he thought, sighing, scratching his chest, inhaling the warm scent of Julie and sex. The question was, *why* had it had been so good?

Or had it only been that good for him?

Kevin rammed his hands through his hair, then pushed out a sigh. One day, *one day,* maybe he was gonna learn that just because an opportunity presents itself, that doesn't mean you hafta act on it.

That maybe being a man meant taking charge of thc situation instead of letting the situation take charge of you. How in the frickin' hell did he keep finding himself in these messes? Even *after* he'd gone straight? Talk about not fair—

"Oh, good, you're awake."

His gaze jerked to Julianne, standing in the doorway. The bad news was she was dressed. And had Pip on her hip.

The good news was she was glowing. And smiling.

Really smiling.

And really, *really* glowing.

Grinning, melting inside, Kevin patted the space beside him. Julie crossed the carpet to awkwardly crawl back onto the bed with the baby in her arms, somehow rearranging some of the pillows so they could snuggle without breaking their backs.

Nice.

"So," he said, holding the two most important females in his life close, "are we okay this morning?"

She lifted her eyes to his. And if he didn't exactly see love there, he at least saw contentment. "We are *very* okay this morning," she said, smiling, pushing herself up to kiss him, and he thought, *That'll do.*

At least, for now.

* * *

Unfortunately, however, afterglows didn't last forever. At least, not with the same intensity. Not that things were bad, exactly, as much as they seemed to be in limbo, Kevin grumpily mused as he pulled up in front of Victor's house several days later, at the end of a very long day in what was turning out to be a very boring job.

The pickup's old engine shuddered into grateful silence when Kevin twisted the key, then sat behind the wheel, trying to rub the kinks out of his neck. He'd originally attributed his grumpiness to not being able to fool around, now that Victor was back. But not really. Okay, sure, he ached like hell for Julianne, but sneaking sex, with her father sleeping right down the hall, wasn't gonna happen. Some things you just don't do. At least, he didn't.

At least, not anymore.

And anyway, otherwise he and Julianne were getting along great. They talked, they kidded around, they played with Pip, they watched dumb reality shows together and yammered all the way through them….

So what was the problem? The problem was that damned limbo thing. Kevin was trying to be patient, he really was, but the fact was that while maybe Julianne was happy with the aimless, drifting thing, Kevin wasn't. He wanted more. He wanted a real life, a real home, a real career.

And he wanted it now. Dammit.

Hence the grumpy mood.

The front door opened, and a barefoot, smiling Julianne tramped down the walk, holding Pip. Kevin pushed open the truck's creaky door and climbed out, making sure to have his own smile in place by the time he walked around to kiss his daughter on her head, shaking his own when she reached out to him.

"Sorry, dumpling, Daddy's hot and sweaty and disgusting."

He tapped the baby on the nose. "Soon as I shower, though, we have a date."

"Dad's grilling steaks," Julianne said, staring at his sweaty chest, the obvious longing in her voice filling him with hope. Or something. "I'll tell him fifteen minutes?"

"Sounds great," he said, weary, and she frowned at him.

"You look ready to drop."

"Swinging a sledgehammer at totally uncooperative plasterboard for eight hours in ninety-five-degree heat'll do that to you."

"Not that that doesn't suck toads," she said, still frowning, "but that's not all, is it?"

Damn women's intuition. "Sure it is. Like you said, I'm just whacked."

"Liar," she said softly, as if she really cared, and Kevin felt a lot like that pulverized plasterboard. Especially when Julianne glanced over her shoulder, then grabbed the front of his sweaty, plaster-dust-caked T-shirt and tugged him close enough to kiss. And not a little peck, either, tongue and everything. Just in time for Ms. Nosybody with the golden retriever to happen by.

Julianne waved to her, unrepentant, then skedaddled back to the house, leaving Kevin more than a little turned on and thoroughly confused.

He stopped in the kitchen only long enough to snag a bottle of iced tea out of the fridge. And, unfortunately, to run into Victor, coming in to get the steaks. "You might not wanna get too close," Kevin said, holding up the tea like a shield, but Victor only gave him a distracted wave and disappeared back outside. Talk about weird, Kevin thought as he slugged back half the bottle, then headed upstairs to detox. Even Julianne had commented on how distracted Victor had seemed since his return. Like something was really bugging him.

A few minutes later Kevin walked out of the bathroom, towel

wrapped around his hips, to find Julianne waiting for him. Dressed. Seated. Intense.

"Where's the Pip?" he asked, yanking clean clothes out of his drawer.

"With Dad. Outside." He dropped the towel. No reaction. On her part, anyway. "I know what your problem is," she said, and Kevin thought, *I sincerely doubt that.*

But no harm in humoring the woman, right? "And what's that?"

"You hate your job. And you hate it here."

He wheeled on her so fast he nearly did himself in with his zipper. "I don't hate it here."

"Yes, you do," she said, with amazing calm for somebody who obviously knew what that meant. Because she was right, even if Kevin hadn't fully admitted the truth to himself until that very moment: that even though he was determined to make the best of it for Pip's sake—for everybody's—now that he'd finally made peace with his family, he really missed them. And going back for Mia's wedding…saying goodbye all over again was gonna blow.

However, his reality-dodging days were over. So, tugging a BoSox T-shirt over his head, he said, "I'll admit the job's makin' me crazy. Grunt work's okay if it's your own project, but this is…"

"Beneath you?"

"No. Just mind-numbing. But I'm sure something better'll come along." He squatted in front of her, taking her hands in his. "It's gonna be okay, honey. I promise."

"You forget who you're talking to," she said sadly, then pushed herself off the bed, as something like fireworks went off inside his chest.

"Holy crap," he breathed, getting to his feet. "You're afraid I won't stick around. And not just because of the baby."

She turned, her mouth twisted. "Go figure," she whispered, then left the room.

Not even fighting the grin, Kevin reached for his watch, just as his cell rang. Figuring it was some Vaccaro or other, he answered without checking the display. "'Lo?"

"Is this Kevin Vaccaro?" said an unfamiliar male voice.

"Yeah, it is. Can I help you?"

"I sure hope so. I got your number from Sandy Epstein, who got it from your brother Rudy. Rumor has it you've got a real feel for working on old houses…?"

Great, Julianne thought at dinner out on the patio, as she leaned over to give Pip a taste of smushed potato salad, hold the relish. Now she had *two* grouchy men clearly determined to keep whatever was making them grouchy under wraps. What was especially annoying—and more than a little disconcerting—was that they both kept shooting her these I'm-so-sorry looks.

What? she wanted to yell at both of them. *Why do you keep looking at me like that?*

And anyway, how dare they steal her thunder? *She* was supposed to be the hugely conflicted one here, the one who still couldn't look at the pool without blushing, the one hyperventilating on a regular basis whenever any thought even remotely connected to Kevin, Pip or the future pranced through her brain. Sharing the angst was not on the agenda.

Especially with her father. Whose funk was beginning to worry more than irritate her. He hadn't even been particularly enthusiastic about her gallery news. Not as though he didn't care, however, as that he simply seemed…preoccupied. Nor had he talked much about his trip. Although, maybe that was just as well. A thousand psychologists under one roof? The entire hotel staff probably needed therapy afterward.

So she did what any woman with a shred of self-preservation

would do: she dug her Bright 'n' Cheerful costume out of mothballs, wriggled into it and pretended that everything was just hunky-dory.

"So," she said to Kevin, just in time to see his guilty look skitter away. "When does your flight leave on Wednesday?"

"Early," Kevin said, pulling a face. A sudden image of that face, sweaty and smug and sated, popped into her head. Then, since thoughts will wander where they will, she got a very nice image of the everything below the face, sans clothes, and very nearly combusted. "I have to be at the airport by six-thirty."

"I'll drive you," her dad said, as though suddenly coming out of his stupor, and *poof* went the naked Kevin.

"You don't have to do that," said the clothed Kevin beside her.

"I'm up, anyway. It's no trouble."

"Thanks, then. Is there any steak sauce?"

"In the fridge," her father said. When Kevin had gone, Julianne leaned across the table to wrap her hand around her dad's arm.

"Hey. Is everything okay?"

"Of course everything's okay." Juice oozed from his steak when he cut into it. Not looking at her. "Why wouldn't it be?"

"You tell me. You've been awfully subdued since you got home."

"Just a lot on my mind, lambchop." Julianne's eyes watered. He hadn't called her that in years. And oddly, she didn't mind.

"That much I figured out. What, is the question."

"It's...personal," Dad said in that I-don't-want-to-worry-you voice, which of course sent terror streaking through her.

"Ohmigod—you're sick! That's it, isn't it? You're dying and you're afraid to tell me!"

Her father frowned at her as though she was speaking in Swahili. "Sick? What on earth would make you think that?" When she glowered at him, he sighed. "I'm fine, honey. I swear. I'm just trying to work through some issues, that's all. Nothing that concerns you, trust me. Now, are you going to tell me what's going on between you and Kevin, or let my jump to my own conclusions?"

And what was left of her appetite went buh-bye.

Through the open kitchen window, Kevin watched Julianne and her father. Heard the concern in her voice, his evasiveness, saw her *Oh, hell* reaction when he asked what was going on between them. Of course she said, "Nothing." No surprise there, seeing as both Victor and Julianne would rather eat rusty nails than be up front with each other. Not that Kevin knew what was eating at Victor any more than Julianne did, but something was obviously troubling the man.

Not that Kevin was exactly being Mr. Lay It All on the Table himself, was he? It wasn't like he got off the phone, walked outside and said, "Guess what?"

Mainly because he had no clue what came after the "Guess what?"

Because, once again, no matter what choice he made, somebody was gonna be hurt. Sure, he talked to Rudy right after he hung up, except all his big brother said was, "You're the only person who can make that decision, bro. But the one thing you don't wanna do is put off tellin' Julianne," at which point Kevin said, "Until I make a decision, I don't have anything to tell her," and Rudy said, "Don't kid yourself, you know damn well what you want to do."

Want to do, yes. Whether he should or not…

Damn it.

Somehow he got through the rest of dinner okay. Although, judging from Julianne's questioning glances every so often, acting probably wasn't his calling. Afterward Victor disappeared into his office and Julianne trailed Kevin into the kitchen, the baby in her arms.

"You up for taking Pip for her walk after we finish? Or are you too tired?"

"No, I'm okay," Kevin said, opening the dishwasher. Dying inside.

"You may not be too tired," she said calmly, one-handedly wetting, then ringing out, a cloth to wipe the baby's hands and face, "but you're a long way from okay. So. Are you going to tell me what's going on? Or are you going to go the macho patronizing route like my father?"

"I heard you guys through the window," he said, loading plates. Stalling. "There's a difference between patronizing and protecting, Julie."

"Not much."

"Then how about patronizing and wanting to keep some things private?"

"I'm his daughter, Kevin. His *grown* daughter. Do you have any idea how it feels, being deliberately shut out of the loop like that? It's like you said—going through hell doesn't make you less able to cope, it makes you stronger. At least, it did me, even if it took me a while to figure that out. So what the hell is up with the don't-fret-your-pretty-little-head about-it routine?

"And," she added, her voice pure don't-mess-with-me, "if you think you just diverted my attention from whatever's going on with you, you're dead wrong. Something happened after we talked before dinner, I can see it in your face. Something I have a pretty good idea concerns me. So spit it out. Now."

The dishes stacked, Kevin slammed the washer door closed, then leaned one hand against the edge of the counter. There was no point in putting off the inevitable. He knew that. And for a moment—one longer than he wanted to admit—the old demons called. Still, once he lifted his eyes to Julianne's, saw the trust in them—in him—they shut up. Just like that.

"You remember when I told you about that dude back East with the big house he's renovating?"

It took a second. But in that second, he saw in her face that he'd apparently made his decision. The baby bounced slightly when she sank onto the nearest kitchen chair. "I heard your cell ring as I left your room. That was him?"

Feeling like scum, Kevin yanked out another chair and swung one leg over it, pulling it close to hers. "Not exactly." He sucked in a breath. "I'd pretty much figured it was a no-go, since he hadn't called. And anyway, I wasn't sure I was qualified, to tell you the truth. Not for a project that big. And I was right. Nat—that's the guy with the house—hired somebody else. But here's the thing."

His gaze steady on hers, his heart whomping in his chest, he said, "The outfit he hired happens to do a lot of work for one of those home makeover shows on TV. We're talking big-time. But the builder lost his right-hand man, something about him having to move outta state because of his wife's job. And this builder, he remembered what Nat had said about me. So he called."

"And offered you a job."

The resignation in Julianne's voice twisted Kevin's heart. His gaze swung to his daughter, who was grunting as she tried to grab her own toes. "It's not totally a done deal. He wants to interview me in person. Although…"

"The interview's just a formality."

Kevin exhaled. "It would seem that way, yeah. And if it was just somebody wanting to spiff up his three-bedroom ranch," he said quickly, "I wouldn't even consider it. But not only is this a dynamite project, it's a chance to work with one of the best construction companies on the East Coast, to learn far more about current restoration methods than I ever would if I stayed here."

His eyes stinging, he said, "Opportunities like this don't come along every day, Julie. Especially for somebody like me."

Kevin leaned over to grab one of the baby's feet. Pip lifted her head and grinned at him. "It's my chance to really be somebody, Julie," he said through a clogged throat. "Somebody my little girl can be proud of, you know?"

Oh God.

Julianne sat there, trying not to grip the baby too tightly. Telling herself, *It's not all about you, cupcake.* The look on Kevin's face...as though he'd just been handed the keys to a Dodge Viper, won the lottery and given fifty-yard-line tickets to the Superbowl, all at the same time...

Oh, *dear* God.

"Wow. You're right, what an incredible opportunity—"

"Julie. Cut the BS."

"What am I supposed to say, Kevin?" she said, keeping her voice level for the baby's sake. "Or did you expect me to throw a fit, cry and scream and say you can't do this, can't take the baby to the other side of the country? *Can't break your promise?* I'm sorry, I'm sorry..." She glanced up at the ceiling, willing her heart to stop battering her sternum, then looked at him again, her insides fisting at his obvious torment. "When would you go?"

"Actually, since I have to go for the wedding anyway..."

Julianne felt the blood drain from her face. "You're not coming back?"

"If I get the job...well." His gaze lifted to hers. "There really wouldn't be much point, would there? Since they want to get started right away."

One of the chair's rungs gouged her spine as she sagged against it. *Breathe,* she thought. *Breathe, dammit—*

"Come with me."

Kevin looked as flabbergasted as she felt. There was a

moment of stunned numbness before panic sliced through her like a hot knife. "*What* did you say?"

"Come with me," he repeated, more strongly, a smile inching across his face. "Not right away, I don't mean that. I'd have to find a place and I know you'd have things to sort out on this end, but…"

"I can't do that!"

"Why not?"

"Ohmigod, Kevin—where would you like me to start?" Her heart was beating so hard she could barely hear herself. "I can't follow you clear to the other side of the country! I just made those contacts for my work, for one thing…and then there's my dad. I have no idea what's going on with him. I couldn't possibly leave now. Besides which…" The panic spread to her lungs. "Kevin," she choked out, "we barely know each other, I don't even know—"

"If you're serious about me," he finished for her.

"If I can ever be that serious again about anybody." Tears burned her eyes. "Which you've known all along."

"I thought…" He stopped, clearly hurt; Julianne's eyes watered.

"I *love* being with you," she whispered. "And why wouldn't I? You're absolutely amazing. But I'm not there yet, Kevin. Not enough to make that kind of commitment. I'm sorry—"

"No, *I'm* sorry," he said, pushing out of the chair. "It was a stupid idea."

"Impulsive," she said gently. "Not stupid. But I'm not. Impulsive, I mean," she said dryly. Pippa started to fuss; Julianne nestled the baby against her chest, rocking her. "Stupid, I don't know about. My God, I dated Gil for almost a year before we even took things to the next level."

She flinched when he wheeled on her. "And yet look how quickly *we* moved to the next level."

"It's not the same thing!"

"Because I'm not Gil?"

"No! *No,* dammit! I mean, yes, of course you're not Gil," she said. "But that's not the problem, believe me, the problem is...*I'm* not who I was before he died. And it's going to take some time to figure who the new Julianne is. And for sure I'm not anywhere near ready to uproot myself when..." She paused, her chest aching. She nuzzled the baby's fuzzy head, holding her tight. "When I'm still not entirely sure if this is just about Pip."

"Don't you *dare* give me that! You know damn well this isn't about her—"

"Then...then it's about sex! It's like you said, y-you don't have to be in love to do the deed with somebody—"

"Things change," he said, his eyes boring into hers, and her breath left her lungs in a ragged little "ohh" as he said, "This is about *us,* Julie. This is about..." She saw him try to steady his breathing. "This is about me fallin' in love with you, even though I told myself *that* was stupid. This is about me wanting you in my life. Wanting us to be a family, to raise Pip together, to maybe have more kids someday—"

"Kevin, you can't possibly be in love with me!" she said, paling. "It's just..."

"What? An infatuation? A fling? You think because I've never been in love before, I don't know what I feel now? You wanna know why I really want to take that job, why my heart skyrocketed when I got that phone call? Because I thought, there's my ticket to making somethin' of myself so Julie'd be proud of me. So by the time you *were* ready, I'd have something worthwhile to offer you."

She was stunned. "You think I'm not already proud of you? Have you forgotten everything I said about how much I admired you?"

"Speaking of bein' patronizing."

"Kevin! What an awful thing to say! For your information, I can count on one hand the number of people I admire."

"And I can count on one *finger* the women I've loved."

Slowly, pieces of the conversation stopped floating around the kitchen and began to settle in her brain. "You're really serious."

Kevin almost laughed. "Ya think? Hell, why do you think this whole thing is tearin' me up inside? Because it's not like I can just take my daughter away and not give a damn about how you feel. For a long time I kept pushing my feelings aside, ignoring them, because..." He lifted his eyes before, on a sharp breath, he lowered them again. "It doesn't matter. What matters is that at least I'm finally bein' honest. I love you, Julie, no matter what. And I love my daughter. And somehow I got this crazy idea that it would be nice if we could all be together."

"On the other side of the country." He looked away. Any second now Julianne's chest was going to cave in. "But...Kevin...what if it never happens for me? What if I'm never ready?"

On a sigh, Kevin dropped back into the chair, leaning forward to tuck her hand, firm on Pip's back, in his. "When I first met you," he said, gently rubbing his thumb over the indentation where her wedding band used to be, "you were like...half the person you are now. It was like you were afraid to move two inches outta your comfort zone. And look at you now, how far you've come. So why would you think this is the end of the road? If you ask me, you've barely gotten started."

After a long moment Julianne shifted the sleepy baby in her arms so she could lift a trembling hand to Kevin's face. It took her three tries before she could speak. "I cannot believe how incredibly blessed I've been," she said, "to have you in my life. To have someone believe in me the way you do."

His Adam's apple bobbing, Kevin covered her hand with his own. "Same here," he said on a long breath.

"I just wish I had half your courage," she whispered, then got the hell out of there before she started sobbing like a damn fool.

Chapter Twelve

Hours of aimless driving later, Kevin finally dragged himself back through Victor's front door. Even though there was no place he wanted to be less. Breathing out a sigh of relief that no one, not even the dog, greeted him, he headed for the kitchen—the half-remodeled kitchen, he noted. The project had coincidentally been abandoned right about the time of Beth's visit. The refinished cabinets looked great, though, Kevin mused as he scoured the fridge for something to drink.

"What's this I hear about you moving back East?"

And so it begins, he thought, twisting off the top to a Gatorade bottle as he turned to face Victor, standing in the doorway with his hands in the pockets of a pair of cargo shorts Kevin guessed were older than the dog. He also guessed whatever had been distracting Julianne's father for the past few days had just taken a back seat to this new development. He didn't look murderous, exactly, but close enough to count.

"I take it you talked to Julie?"

"I wormed it out of her. She's absolutely devastated."

"Yeah, well, that makes two of us," Kevin muttered, then met the older man's unyielding gaze. "I feel like hell about this, Victor. I swear. But I have to do what's best for my daughter in the long run."

"And you think this job is it?"

"If it pans out—yeah, it is. And you know it's not some snap decision. Maybe I didn't think anything would come of it, but...but I guess on some level I'd thought about it more than I'd realized."

"With no consideration for my daughter, obviously."

"Dammit, Victor," Kevin said wearily. "I asked her to come with me, what more do you want?"

"You *what?*"

The bottle halfway to his mouth, Kevin ducked his head, eyes narrowed. "She didn't tell you?"

"No." Kevin couldn't tell if Victor was more upset with him or Julianne. "So you two *are* involved."

"Yeah. We are. Although apparently *I* am far more than she is." He set the bottle on the counter, then leaned back against it, fingers stuffed in his front pockets. "Which probably isn't nearly the disappointment to you that it is to me. I know I'm not exactly your ideal candidate."

"But you assured me—"

"I honest to God didn't think I had a chance, Victor. I never said I didn't want one." His gaze remained steady on the older man's. "If it was offered."

A beat or two passed before Victor pulled out a kitchen chair and sat, his arms folded across his chest. "Sit down, son."

"Thanks, but—"

"Sit, dammit." When, reluctantly, Kevin obeyed, Victor looked him straight in the eye. "I've got no beef with you, Kevin."

"Oh, really?" he said, crossing his arms. "When did I pass muster?"

"The clincher? When I walked in here just now and realized you weren't drunk. Or worse."

Kevin's brows slammed together. "Gee, thanks for the vote of confidence."

"After what I went through with Robyn," Victor said sharply, "I'd rather be cynical than gullible. However," he said, cutting Kevin off, "hard as this is for me to admit...you're obviously the exception. In fact, you're a good kid."

"I'm not a kid, Victor. And I've got the battle scars to prove it."

"No," the older man said, one side of his mouth lifting. "No, you're not. And in other circumstances...I'd be okay about you and Julie. Eventually. But right now?" He shook his head. "She's not ready, Kevin. At least, to make the kind of commitment that involves leaving everything she knows. Uprooting her now could destroy whatever progress she's made."

"Progress even she admits happened since I came on the scene."

Victor stared him down for several moments before his lips curved. "You're still one cocky SOB, aren't you?"

"Sorry. It's genetic." Gus had leaned against Kevin's thigh; he plowed his fingers into the dog's ruff. "I know Julie's not ready," he said softly. "And I would've never pushed her if this hadn't come up. But how else was I s'posedta let her know how serious I was?"

"And how serious are you?"

Kevin snorted a laugh through his nose. "Serious enough that it's killin' me, the thought of not being with her. That whatever worries her, worries me. Like you, for instance."

Clearly surprised by the abrupt switch, Victor frowned. "Me?"

"Yeah, you...who's been acting weirder than weird since you got back from that conference. Julie even threw out your behavior as one of the reasons why she can't go with me."

"You think I'm standing in her way?"

"You wanna know the truth?" Kevin said, thinking, *What the hell, how much worse can things get?* "I think you've been standing in her way for months. Not that you meant to. I know how much you love your daughter. And seeing the way the two of you were there for each other when it really mattered... That's what family's all about, right? But as long as you kept Julianne safe, she had no reason to see what else was goin' on in the world, did she?"

Victor unfolded his arms to straighten a crooked place mat in front of him. "Forget fixing up houses," he said, glancing at Kevin. "You should help me write my next book."

"If the price is right, you're on."

Julianne's father laughed out loud, but only for a second. "Over the years," he said, "I've probably worked with thousands of people. But I can honestly say I've never met anyone with more innate integrity than you. Don't get me wrong, you're still a pain in the ass. But you're the damn finest pain in the ass I've ever met." A brief, contrite look crossed his face. "And I apologize for forgetting, when we first met, that facts in a computer printout can't possibly give an accurate picture of the real person."

When Kevin found his voice, he said, "Apology accepted. Even though I understand that you were only trying to protect Pippa."

Victor regarded him for a moment, then said, "Did you know Julie can't have any more children?"

It took a second before Victor's words sank in. There'd been this one time, when he was a kid, when he'd gotten creamed by some enormous dude who missed the memo that they were supposed to be playing *touch* football. This felt five times worse. "Why the hell didn't she tell me?" he whispered.

"I suppose because whatever happened, she didn't want sympathy for *her* to influence your decisions."

Feeling sick to his stomach, Kevin said, "Which only goes to prove she's a lot stronger than you give her credit for. Or for that matter—" he grabbed his half-finished drink off the counter, thinking one more bombshell today and he'd be dead "—she gives herself."

Victor stood, silently regarded Kevin for several seconds, then left the room, his shoulders drooping like his pain weighed ten tons.

Julianne had known it would be hell, leaving Pip behind with her father all afternoon. But better to start the separation process early, right? Besides, keeping busy, on the move, was her only shot at staying sane. So she spent most of the day before Kevin and Pip's departure carting boxes of Fairy Tails stuff to the two galleries. After that, she wandered around the mall for a while and bought nothing, then went to a not-very-good movie, where she ate eight bucks' worth of popcorn for dinner. Anything to avoid...everything.

Especially saying goodbye.

And hadn't she had enough of those to last a lifetime? she thought when she finally let herself into the house after Pip's bedtime. Patting herself on the back for not crying even once all day, she stood for a moment in the entry hall, waiting for the comforting, familiar sounds and sights and smells to lull her into feeling safe.

Except then Kevin popped out of nowhere, like a frickin' ghost—with an attitude—and she thought, *Hah.*

"Where were you?"

"Out," she said, dumping her purse on the hall table. Clinging to the didn't-cry-all-day thing. "Living my life. Pretending to be normal."

"Punishing me."

"No," she said on an exhaled breath, looking at herself in the mirror over the table. Makeup gone, hair straggly, linen blouse wilted. Blech. Then she shifted her gaze to his reflection. Blech, again, but for different reasons. "You're doing what you have to do, Kevin." She turned, facing all that goodness and strength and courage, and thought, *Why can't I be like that?* "And so am I."

He nodded, looking like hell, and it occurred to her a weaker woman would have caved, just to keep him from looking so miserable.

However.

Shoulders squared, she asked, "Are you all ready to g-go?"

"Mostly. Your dad said he'd send most of Pip's things on ahead later." His smile looked totally fake. "How on earth can someone who isn't even six months old yet have so much stuff?"

"Just wait until she turns sixteen," Julianne said, smiling, as well, feeling like the Grinch's demented cousin.

"Dammit, Julie," Kevin whispered, and a second later she was in his arms.

Caving.

They made love for hours, in his bed this time, nobody giving a damn whether Julianne's father knew or not. Victor was a smart guy, he could put two and two together.

Not that Kevin had known himself that they'd end up like this, considering how Julianne had kept her distance all day. Or that anger would fuel the first round or two of their lovemaking, that they'd use their bodies to convey all the stuff they couldn't say. The last time, however, had clearly been about regret and heartache. And, yeah, tenderness. The kind of tenderness a man feels a lot more than he might admit, when it's the right woman. Now, finally spent, they lay spooned together, breathing in tandem, their hands linked on the mattress in front of her breasts, until he kissed her shoulder and said, "I really have to pack."

"Because God forbid a man ever do something before the last minute," she said, obviously smiling. Obviously heartsick.

After a kiss that would lead to more hanky-panky if he wasn't careful, Kevin got up and pulled on his jeans, then tossed his duffel bag onto the foot of the bed. On her side, the sheet pulled up, a very bedheaded Julianne watched him cross to the chest of drawers. "I'm sorry," she said at last, and he thought, *Here it comes.*

"For what?"

"You know what."

"And I knew it was a long shot," he said, cramming his T-shirts into the bag. "So don't you dare do a guilt trip on yourself." He turned away to yank open the top drawer to the bureau. "There's nothing to be sorry about, okay?"

"It's just that Dad—"

"Damn it, Julianne," he sighed out, then looked at her. "At least be honest enough to stop hiding behind your father. I get that you feel you owe him for being there for you when your life took a header—"

"It's more than that, Kevin—"

"I *know* it's more than that. That's my point. Look, I've got no issues with the two of you being close. I've got no issues with your father, period. He's been through hell. You both have. But it's like…I dunno. Like the two of you seem to think as long as you stay inside this little world you've made with each other, nothing else bad can happen."

Color flooded her cheeks. "You make it sound as though we never leave the house!"

"A prison doesn't hafta have four walls, Julie. And take it from somebody who knows—the hardest ones to break out of are the ones you make for yourself." He swallowed. "And you and I both know whatever's keepin' you from coming with me has nothing to do with your father."

"And I said I wasn't ready."

"Sorry, Julie, but you don't make love like a woman who's not ready. Just like one who's scared to admit she is."

He saw her eyes go shiny before, wordlessly, she got up, yanked the top sheet off the bed to wrap around herself, and left the room.

Good going, bonehead, Kevin thought as he slammed shut the empty drawer, then stormed to the closet to grab the polo shirt and pair of khakis off their hangers. Okay, so he'd had to get that off his chest. And Julianne needed to hear it. But maybe one of these days he'd figure out how to get his point across without pissing off the people who most mattered to him. Not that he was holding his breath or anything.

This wasn't at all how he'd imagined their last night together. In his head, he'd seen them acting like mature adults, talking about Pippa, maybe some kissing and hugging at the end. Instead, he'd slammed the ball back into Julianne's court hard enough to knock her out.

He sank onto the edge of the mattress, his head in his hands. How had this happened? Why was it that the more he tried to fix stuff, the more screwed-up it got? Why was life so damned *hard?*

His packing done except for his bathroom crap, which he'd gather the next morning, Kevin dumped the unzipped duffel on the floor, next to the baby bag he'd already packed for Pip earlier. By rights, he thought as he crept into Pip's room, he should be a lot more nervous about a cross-country flight with a baby, although he had had the occasional panic of how to handle potty breaks for himself with a nearly six-month-old baby girl.

He stood over Pip's crib, watching her sleep. In the last week she'd figured out how to flip from her back to her tummy. Julianne had been so excited that night when he'd gotten back from work she'd barely been able to contain herself.

"Come see what our girl learned to do today!" she'd said, tugging him into the living room, where Pippa obliged, again and again, laughing her little belly laugh. And every time she flipped over, those big blue eyes, filled with unconditional trust and love, would zing to Julianne's. Then Julianne had gathered her into her arms, the baby immediately molding herself to the one human being who'd been the biggest constant in her life.

In response, Julianne had laid her cheek on top of Pip's head, breathing out a long, slow sigh of contentment, and Kevin had realized at that moment that his daughter had literally saved her aunt's life.

And that was before he'd known Julie couldn't have kids of her own.

"Ah-ghhsht?"

He looked down; Pip had shifted onto her side, regarding him sleepily in the light spearing through her open door.

"Hey, peanut," Kevin whispered, cupping her head, and she smiled, showing off a brand-new tooth. Now on her back, she thumped her feet a couple of times, the smile broadening into that same no-holds-barred, trusting look she'd given Julianne that night. An absolute conviction that Daddy knew best.

For the first time, the full impact of what that meant hit him like a sledgehammer.

Throwing common sense to the four winds, Kevin picked her up and lowered himself into the glider, indulging himself in the sweetness of rocking his baby girl back to sleep.

Julianne lay awake virtually the entire night, only to wake up out of a fitful doze just as Kevin and her father left. Dad's car was barely out of the driveway before she let out a sob; Gus rushed—for Gus—over to console her, licking the tears off her face and making little worried whines in his throat.

How many times, Julianne wondered as she lay there in a pool of tears and snot, could a person's heart break before it couldn't be fixed anymore?

At long last, however, she stopped blubbering, hauled her sorry self out of bed and padded downstairs to the kitchen. There was just enough coffee left in the pot to fill her mug; she noticed Kevin's, one of her tuxedoed hounds, and her eyes filled all over again. That he wasn't here. That he hadn't taken it with him. That he had taken Pip.

On another pathetic little sniffle, she dropped into a kitchen chair, watching the sky lighten and forcing herself to face her new reality.

No more changing diapers. No more soft, sweet-smelling little girl in her arms. No more swearing when a stroller wheel got caught in a sidewalk crack. No more gummy smiles, or baby belly laughs, or watching Pip discover her toes or fingers or what happens when you blow sweet potatoes through your lips.

No more moonlit swims, naked or otherwise. Or watching Kevin do the spastic turkey dance with his daughter. No more pep talks. Or sentences that started with, "I know this is none of my business, but..."

Or that look in those calm, warm, caramel eyes that melted her bones.

And, dammit, her heart.

The garage door groaned open; Julianne quickly wiped her eyes and blew her nose, determined not to give her father anything more to fret about. He still hadn't told her what was bothering him, but the least she could do was not add to his worries—

Wait—who was he talking to? Julianne stumbled upright, grabbing for the chair's back to keep from losing her balance as her father entered the kitchen, the baby in his arms. Pip saw Julianne, squealed, then stuffed three fingers in her mouth.

"Kid's starving," Victor said mildly as Julianne gawked from Pip to him and back again.

"I don't...I don't understand..."

Victor deposited Pip in her high chair, strapped her in, then dug a sealed envelope out of his pants pocket which he handed to Julianne. "From Kevin. And no, I don't know what it says. Not entirely, anyway. I had no idea when we loaded up this morning that Pip would be coming back with me." He paused. "But then, I'm not entirely sure Kevin knew, either."

As she stared at the envelope, her heart galloping, Dad put his arm around her. "I may not know everything, but I do know I've never seen anybody more in love than Kevin is with you."

Julianne tore her eyes from the letter to meet her father's gaze. "And you're...okay with that?"

Dad smiled. "If Kevin doesn't care whether I am or not, why should you?"

Knees shaking, Julianne carried the note outside, where the birds were singing their fool heads off, to collapse into one of the patio chairs underneath a lavender sky.

Julie,

It's, like, three in the morning. I haven't slept at all. I'm guessing you're probably awake, too, but I don't want to talk about this, because I don't want to give you the chance to say no. To talk me out of what I'm about to say.

A lot of people are gonna think I'm an idiot, especially considering everything I said about how I'd never walk away from my own daughter. But the way I figure it, no matter which door I choose the damn tiger's gonna eat me anyway. In the end, I decided to go with whatever's gonna hurt the fewest people in the long run. At least, that's what I'm hoping.

We've been all over why I feel I need to grab this opportunity, so I won't go there again. Same with why you didn't feel you could come with me. Whether you understand why I made the decision I did, I don't know. But I do understand why you made yours. I swear.

However, you've raised Pip since she was born, honey.

To her, you're not her aunt, you're her mom, and I know you love her every bit as much as any mother could love a kid. Maybe more, because of all the stuff that happened to you. And in the end, I just couldn't see splitting the two of you up. Especially after what your Dad told me, about how you can't have more kids—

"What?"

Her heart pounding, Julianne blinked furiously against the haze of fury blurring Kevin's words. How could Dad *do* that, when she'd made him swear not to tell Kevin the truth…?

And please don't be mad at him. He only wanted to make sure I had all the facts before I made a final decision.

Although, don't think for a minute this means I'm just abandoning my daughter. I have no idea how things are going to work out, but trust me, Pip's gonna know who her daddy is.

And okay, since you can't yell at me, either…I have to tell you, I think what you said about only getting one shot at love is totally bogus. But you know, maybe your not being ready really means I'm *not* the right person. I don't know, I could be totally off base, but that's what comes to me. And I'm sorry if it felt like I was pressuring you, which is kind of a messed-up way of showing somebody you love them. But not nearly as messed up as taking away the one thing that's most important to them.

I've left addresses and phone numbers, etc., on a separate sheet of paper. And tell your dad, if he's still serious about the twenty grand, to just put it toward Pip's college fund. That's what I would've done with it anyway.

All I want is to do what's best for everybody. Which isn't always easy, you know?

Take care. Give Pip a kiss from me and tell her I'll see her soon.

Kev

His heart in pieces, Victor stood at the patio door, feeding Pip her morning bottle as he watched Julie read the letter. When she finished, she carefully lowered the paper to the tempered-glass table, rocked back and forth for a few seconds, then simply…fell apart. Victor shoved open the patio door and stormed outside, lowering the baby into her seat before gathering his grief-racked daughter in his arms.

"Julie, honey—what on earth did he say?"

Victor thought she might have said, "Read it yourself." It was hard to tell with all the crying. So he did. And the minute he finished, he knew two things: one, that Kevin Vaccaro was one remarkable young man, and two, that his daughter was hopelessly, helplessly in love with him, too.

Even if she didn't have a clue what to do about it.

Welcome to my world, Victor thought on a sigh, as his little girl keened in his arms.

Julianne stopped pacing in front of her father's desk in his office long enough to glare at him through swollen eyes. Hours after the tears and the hiccups, the intermittent growls of despair, followed by slogging through the roughly five gazillion emotions left in the wake of Kevin's sacrifice, one stood head and shoulders above the rest:

Rage.

"You had no right to tell him that, Dad! None!"

"I just thought he should have all the facts, that's all."

"Knowing damn well what he'd do if he did! Why do you

think I chose *not* to tell Kevin I couldn't have children? As if things weren't hard enough without your manipulating things!"

Her father leaned back in his chair, his hands folded over his stomach, an inscrutable smile tugging at his mouth. "You don't think Kevin wouldn't have done what he did anyway? Even if he hadn't known?"

Okay, all of this was giving her a serious headache. "Obviously *you* didn't. But that's not the point. The point is…oh, *hell!*" Like a puppet whose strings had been cut, Julianne sagged into the wing chair at the corner of her father's desk, forking her tangled bangs away from her face as a fresh round of tears threatened. "I have no idea what the point is anymore."

"Of course you do," her dad said gently. "And when the shock's blown over, you need to look it straight in the eye and deal with the fact that you've fallen hook, line and sinker for somebody in such a short time, and it scares the hell out of you."

"That's not true—"

"Julie."

Tears spilled over. "I hate you," she mumbled.

Her father waited. She sighed.

"Okay, so I've fallen for the turkey. But I can't…"

"What?" he said, handing her the tissue box. She snatched one out, sending the box clattering to the floor and Gus—who'd been sleeping beside the desk—shooting a foot in the air.

"I just thought I'd have more time to think it through, for one thing."

"So I gathered. But the longer you think about it, the more reasons you'll come up why it would never work."

"And this is a bad thing, why? Yeesh, Dad—whose side are you on?"

"Yours. Always. So what are some of these reasons?"

She sniffled. "Got your shrink hat on, do ya?"

"Just answer the question, Miss Smarty-Pants."

So she did. Rattled 'em off quicker than an overachieving fourth-grader did the times tables. About how she wasn't ready, it happened too fast, they probably weren't suited…each sounding more lame than the last. Except for:

"And how can I leave *you?*"

After a moment, her father got up and walked over to the window overlooking his beloved garden, his arms folded over his chest. "Beth was with me in Maui," he said quietly, and something inside Julie went *ding-ding-ding.*

"And…does that have anything to do with why you've been so grumpy since you came back?"

He turned, every line in his face screaming, *You're not gonna like this.* "What I've been, honey, is tortured. Torn between my duty as a father and an ever-increasing conviction that I'm not doing either of us any favors by constantly ignoring my own life. My own opportunities. Beth has been incredibly patient with me—more patient than I even realized, or probably deserved—but she's not going to wait forever. Not this time." His smile stretched. "Especially since, at our ages, forever isn't as long as it used to be."

"Dad? What are you saying?"

"I'm saying…you're the only one who can decide what to do about Kevin. I can't protect you either way. Nor should I. Yes, I know I played the meddling card about your condition, but that was before—" he sighed "—before Kevin made me realize how wrong it was to keep running interference for you. Especially since you've come so far these past few weeks…" Her father's eyes glittered; Julianne's filled in response. "As they say, my work here is done." He hauled in a breath. "So now it's my turn. I'm selling the house and moving to Virginia to be with Beth."

Julianne's jaw dropped. "How can you sell the house? It's…it's…"

"A house, honey. Not a life. So. You can stay in Albuquerque or come with me or go live on the moon, but this being-glued-to-each-other business has got to end."

"You're shoving me out of the nest?"

"As hard as I can, sweetheart."

"Ohmigod," Julianne whispered, waiting for this second blow to register. But oddly it didn't. At least, not in the way she would have expected. Instead, her father's announcement seemed to unclog something inside her—him, too, judging from his expression—leaving her feeling suddenly as free as that proverbial, de-nested bird.

A lot freer, anyway. There was still all the Kevin/Pip junk to clear out.

But that could wait, she thought as she catapulted out of the chair to throw her arms around her father, blubbering about how thrilled she was, that Beth was the greatest, that she was so happy for him.

"You really mean it?"

"I really do. I'm only sorry..." She shook her head, sniffling. "I'm sorry you felt you couldn't move forward before this. Because of me."

"It wasn't you, lambchop. Not really. It never was." He smiled, touching her hair. "It was me. It's like I say in my books—no one else is responsible for our happiness. Or lack thereof. And," he said with a pointed look, "letting fear rule our lives is a surefire way to miss out on way too much."

With her hands clamped around her father's arms, Julianne made a face at him. "You do realize your decision to be with Beth has nothing to do with me and Kevin?"

"I know. But damned if I'm going to let you use me to hide behind."

"But..." Julianne bit her lip. "Sorry to bring this up now, but we really have to talk custody arrangements."

Her father frowned. "There's nothing to discuss. Pip stays with you—"

"Not Pip. Gus."

Hearing his name, the Lab chugged over to her, his tail wagging.

"There's nothing to discuss," Dad said, squatting to hug his furry friend. "The dog goes with me. And now if you'll excuse me, I have a phone call to make." At Julianne's frown, he added, "I thought it prudent to not put out the For Sale sign until after I'd told you."

"Good thinking," Julianne said. He was on the phone with a real-estate agent before she left the room.

At some point the ramifications of her father's announcement were going to sink in—that she had to find someplace else to live, for one thing. And a potting studio. Not that this was a problem—Gil had been very well insured, and they'd had some investments, and there was the money from the sale of the Seattle house, which would come within a few weeks. And now that her career looked like it might be getting back on track…

Julianne had made it as far as the living room, where the baby monitor sat on the coffee table, sneering at her.

Right.

It wasn't that she couldn't handle being a single mother. Or whatever. Not only did she feel reasonably confident in her nurturing abilities, she was also fortunate enough to be able to afford help. It was just…

She perched on the edge of one of the sofas, rubbing her palms over and over her thighs. It was just that, Kevin's noble act notwithstanding, it wasn't right. Pip needed her father. Of that much Julianne was absolutely certain.

Whether *she* needed Pip's father…

The ache of need, of loss, of something so scary she hardly dared look it in the face, walloped her hard enough to make her gasp. Tears stung her eyes as, for the first time in forever, she heard herself praying, "Oh, dear God—what am I supposed to do?"

Closing her eyes, Julianne sat very still, for a very long time, just…listening.

Until, eventually, she had her answer.

Chapter Thirteen

The votes were in, and the verdict was unanimous: Kevin was an idiot.

The comments had ranged from "What were you *thinking*, man?" from assorted brothers to "Of all the boneheaded things you've ever done, this beats 'em all" from his father to something in Hungarian from his mother that he'd *never* heard before. But he was betting it wasn't good.

Not that Kevin wasn't having second thoughts himself. Hell, try a hundred. When the plane landed in Cleveland for his layover, he was sorely tempted to take the next flight back to Albuquerque, he missed his daughter so bad.

Then there was Julianne. Oh God, Julianne... *Her* he was missing so much he thought he'd lose his mind. What little was left after his family had gotten done making mincemeat of it, anyway.

"What was I s'posedta do, Pops?" he said at supper that night, just the three of them in the kitchen that always smelled of baking and butter-fried onions, in the two-story, brick foursquare he'd grown up in. "Drag Julianne back here against her will?"

His father's thick white hair and full beard notwithstanding, at the moment there was nothing even remotely jolly in Benny Vaccaro's expression. "Of course not. But for God's sake, Kevin, how could you leave your own kid behind?"

"You think this isn't killing me? You think I don't have a hole the size of the Grand Canyon in the center of my chest? But Julie..." His throat too swollen to eat his mother's stuffed paprika chicken, Kevin shook his head. "I couldn't take the baby away from her, Pop. I just couldn't. If you'd seen them together..." He shook his head, repeating, "I just couldn't."

That got the classic exchanged glance between his parents. Then his father said, "This Julie, she must be somethin' else."

They already knew her backstory, about Gil, about Julianne's mother. And of course Robyn—and since his oldest brother had ended up marrying the sister of one of his old girlfriends, there wasn't much they could say about that. About her work—he'd brought back a dancing pig spoon rest for his mother. She not only loved it, she practically became unhinged with excitement when Ma learned there was a matching canister set.

"Yeah," Kevin said. "She is. Now can we please change the subject or I'm never gonna get my food down." He sent a half-assed smile in his mother's direction. "And it's much too good to let go to waste."

Magda Vaccaro reached over and squeezed his hand, hard enough that her fake fingernails dug a little into his skin. To describe his mother—still ready for her big-top spotlight after all these years—could never do her justice. All Kevin knew was that underneath the big hair and the dramatic makeup and the too-tight clothes that used to embarrass the hell out of him and his brothers—while making their house *the* place for the neighborhood kids, and their pervy fathers, to hang out—beat the heart of the warmest, most genuinely loving woman on the planet. Next to Julianne, of course. "So. You go to see zis man tomorrow about ze job?"

"Yeah," Kevin sighed out. At least this part of things, the folks were okay with. More than okay, they were thrilled. Unfortunately, the rest of Kevin's life being in the crapper was kinda dulling the thrill factor for himself. Without Julie and Pip, what was the point? "I'm driving down to meet this Joe Banyon at the Epstein house to talk things over, then Mia's insisting I spend the next two nights with her and Grant. You're coming down Friday night, right?"

Kevin's father pretended to look put out, but Kevin knew he was secretly beside himself about walking his only daughter down the aisle. "Mia says we gotta. For the rehearsal dinner and all that—"

"Oh, stop being such a pain in ze butt," his mother said, blue-collar New England contaminating but not overpowering her Hungarian accent, and Kevin thought about how not-from-the-same-galaxy different his family was from Julie and Victor, and thought, *Maybe it's for the best, that it didn't work out.* Except then his mother said something about Mia's über-Greenwich mother-in-law-to-be being a "hoot," and it occurred to him if his mother and Bitsy Braeburn could find common ground, there was hope for anybody.

Which he didn't find at all comforting.

"Don't forget to pick up your tux before you go," his mother said as the phone rang. "Since ze Fourth is ze next day, zey won't be open." While Kevin thought assorted bah-humbug thoughts about weddings in general, his father turned around to pluck the phone off the counter, frowning at the caller ID for a second before answering.

"Yeah, this is him," he said, poker-faced, then got up, slamming open the screen door to carry the phone out onto the back porch. Kevin briefly thought about the tree house in the huge old oak in the yard, pockmarked with the gouges and dents made by six kids, umpteen grandkids. The thought of Pip maybe never getting to add her own—

"See? I don't forget which is your favorite," his mother said, setting a still-warm cherry strudel in front of him, a made-in-heaven combination of flaky and gooey, buttery sweet and acid tart, and he was catapulted back to that breathtakingly brief period in his life he could still call innocent. That his parents had never written him off…

Impulsively, he grabbed his mother's hand and kissed her knuckles. Although obviously startled for a second, she quickly recovered, even if her eyes did seem a bit shinier than usual. "Is okay," she whispered, bending over to kiss Kevin's forehead before handing him a large knife to serve the strudel.

Julianne would go nuts for this, Kevin thought, miserable.

Clearly, Julianne had boarded her flight in Albuquerque and landed in *The Twilight Zone.* Because on the other side of the security checkpoint in the Springfield/New Haven airport, Santa Claus was holding a sign that read JULIANNE AND PIPPA!!!

And beside him, in snug, leopard-print capris and four-inch mules, yelling, "Zere zey are!" Dolly Parton with an Eastern European accent.

Except an instant later Santa Claus relieved her of the baby carrier and Dolly embraced her—and her carryon, and the baby bag—in a cloud of perfume that was at once much too strong and completely perfect, and Julianne felt her eyes sting in immediate and profound relief.

"You are Julianne, right?" Santa Claus said. From the depths of Dolly's bosom, Julianne let out a weary, if slightly strangled laugh.

"Yes."

"It occurred to me, maybe I should check," Santa said with a deep chuckle. "Benny Vaccaro," he said, extending his hand. "And the woman squeezin' the life outta ya's Magda, Kevin's mother."

Magda let go long enough for Julianne to shake Benny's hand, only he, too, said, "Oh, what the hell?" and pulled her into a one-armed hug that nearly knocked her off balance. Then smooth, long-nailed hands clasped her shoulders while a concerned, false-eyelashed gaze meshed with hers. "Let me guess—ze flight sucked?"

Julianne let out a weary laugh. "Actually, the flights were okay. Sitting on the runway for two hours in St. Louis, however—*that* sucked."

But by this time Magda had let go to spring her newest granddaughter from her carrier and Julianne might as well have been invisible.

"Would you look at zis *angel?* She looks exactly like Kevin did as zis age, doesn't she, Benny?"

"What are ya talking about, Mag?" Benny said good-naturedly, giving his granddaughter a besotted smile. "She don't look a thing like Kev. I remember Kev as a baby." He turned to Julianne, his eyes twinkling. "Ugliest kid you ever saw, swear to God. And let's get goin', ladies, the traffic's gonna be a bitch this time of day."

"Not true!" Magda said, her heels click-clicking on the concourse as they headed, Julianne presumed, to the baggage claim. "Not about ze traffic, about Kevin being ugly. Ve had six of ze most beautiful babies you could efer hope to see," she said to Julianne after playfully smacking Benny's arm. "Now," she said, giving Pippa a huge, lipsticky kiss on her cheek, "we hef beautiful *grandbabies.*"

Amazingly, Pippa seemed to take her grandmother's overly exuberant, nonstop chatter in stride. Aside from the occasional "Who *is* this woman?" frown in Julianne's direction, that is.

At some point, Julianne was going to realize the enormity of what she'd done—and had yet to do—and probably keel over in shock. But from the moment she got her "answer," it was as if something far bigger than herself was guiding her actions, and she had no choice but to go along for the ride.

And trust that if it felt right, it was.

"So. You got much baggage?" Benny Vaccaro said beside her.

"The baby's stroller and one small bag for me, that's it. Did you… You did tell Kevin I was coming, didn't you?"

When she'd called them last night, and Benny had told her Kevin was there, she'd fully intended to ask if she could talk to him. But that voice or force or whatever it was said, as clearly as an actual person talking to her, "No, you need to *go* to him." Real pain in the can, that voice. In any case, right on the spot she'd said, "I'll be there tomorrow," but she'd never told Kevin's father *not* to tell him she was coming.

Apparently, judging from their shared glance, she should have.

"He doesn't know we're here?" she said on a squeak.

Benny grinned. "Nah. And anyway, he's already down at his sister's in Connecticut. So we figured you could surprise him at the wedding."

Julianne stopped so abruptly a college kid behind her nearly tripped over her, muttering, "Dude—watch out!"

"The wedding?" Oh, hell. In her zeal to follow The Voice's commands, she'd somehow spaced out on the wedding. And apparently The Voice hadn't deemed a reminder necessary. Now, however, it all came rushing back. "I can't go to the wedding!"

"Why not?"

"I wasn't invited? I've got nothing to wear? I don't have a gift?" She caught her breath. "Causing a scene at other people's weddings is hugely tacky?"

"If you wanna talk to Kevin, you got no choice," Benny said, still mildly. "By the way—he got the job, no sweat. So good news all around, right?"

No wonder Kevin had taken to drink. His parents were completely cracked.

"But ve hef to go up a day early, enyway," Magda said, "so ve'll take you." She beamed. "Finally, efter four boys, I get to be a muzzer of ze bride! Is zat a kick in ze pants, or what?"

"Go with you? No, no—I can't possibly intrude—"

"Obviously," Kevin's father said behind her as they reached the baggage area, "you don't know our family. Intrudin's what we do best."

"You said it, buddy," Magda said, smiling at Pippa, and Julianne sighed. Yep. The Vaccaros were totally nuts.

In a weirdly adorable sort of way.

"Uncle Kevin! Uncle Kevin! You're here, you're here, you're here!"

He'd no sooner stepped out of his mother's fifteen-year-old Taurus when a curly-headed blond sprite in a retina-searing blue sundress tore out of the front door of her daddy's gray stone, twenties-vintage, totally kick-ass eight-bedroom house tucked away in a wooded pocket of Greenwich. It was hard to believe he'd just been here last November, at the tail end of his drifting phase, staying with Mia while she helped her unofficial godchild recover from her mother's sudden death a few months before.

"Hey, chipmunk!" Kevin said as Haley wrapped her arms around his neck and gave him a huge hug and noisy kiss on his cheek, and his heart warped, whining at him that he'd made the wrong decision. Oh, well, too late now—

"Kevin!"

Smiling, Kevin set Haley down to shake hands with Mia's fiancé, Grant Braeburn. Kevin had liked Grant—who'd been divorced from Haley's mother for more than a year at the time of her accident—from the start, despite the man's being insanely rich. And better-looking than a straight man had any right to be. Even Mia said that, in the right lighting—and the wrong mood—Grant looked just like one of those dark, brooding hunks from the cover of a romance novel. But with shorter hair.

Nothing brooding about him today, though, as he gave Kevin's hand a brief, firm shake, a huge smile stretched across his face. The smile of a man about to marry the woman he loved, Kevin thought over a stab of out-and-out envy, with a little bitterness thrown in for good measure.

Hey. You're the one who left, numbskull. You could've stayed, given her a chance to catch up. But no...

"Mia's in the guesthouse, spiffing it up for your parents. Your room's the second one on the right upstairs, if you want to unpack first."

Unpack. Right. As in, hang up the plastic-covered tux, toss the duffel in a corner. "Thanks."

Shortly afterward he found his four-years-older sister—barefoot, long hair half up, half down, wearing baggy shorts and a sports bra—muttering at a flower arrangement on the coffee table of the two-bedroom guesthouse. Kevin released a sigh of gratitude that, as far as he could tell, the prospect of becoming a wealthy woman hadn't changed her. That she was still just Mia.

"Boo."

Mia spun around, then let out a whoop of joy before strangling him in a hug. Ten minutes later they were walking in one of the many informal gardens flanking the house, this time of year crowded with old roses and a whole bunch of perennials Kevin didn't know the names of. "Okay, spill," she said the moment they'd gotten away. "And leave nothing out."

So he spilled, and she listened, and—naturally—tossed in her two cents, which was already up to at least a buck fifty before

Kevin said, "It's less than two days before your wedding—aren't you supposed to be terrorizing the florist or caterer or somebody?"

Laughing, she plucked some kind of flower off a low-hanging branch and threw it at him. "One of the perks of being a party planner is having an entire staff to do the terrorizing for me. All I have to do is put on the pretty white dress and show up."

"Still. I remember our sisters-in-law. Every one of 'em was a mess. You seem so…calm."

"It's a wedding, Kev," Mia said, grinning, "not a nuclear summit. If a hurricane blew through tonight and destroyed everything, it still couldn't touch the *reason* for the wedding, could it? Oh God, Kev—I'm so damn happy, I can't *stand* it."

"And I'm happy for you, Mimi. I really am."

"Thanks," she said, tears glittering in her eyes. Then she swung one arm around his shoulders. "Oh, Kev…things do have a way of falling into place, they really do. And you've come such a long way. No, I swear—I'm not sure you give yourself enough credit for everything you've overcome. Damn, I'm proud of you."

Since Mia was one of the people he'd most felt he'd let down, her praise now was a sorely needed balm. "So you don't think I blew it?"

"What I think," she said gently, "is that there's no such a thing as an unsolvable problem. Julianne sounds like a perfectly reasonable human being. I'm sure you could work out some sort of joint-custody arrangement. Maybe it wouldn't be ideal," she said when he grunted, "but you seem to think this is all or nothing. It doesn't have to be that way."

"It does with Julianne. Ow!" he said, palming the back of his head where his sister had smacked it. "What was that for?"

"For wallowing in self-pity instead of doing something about it. The woman hasn't molecularly deconstructed into another dimension, for God's sake! Do you have any idea the balls it took for you to decide your daughter might be better off with her? So, what? Did you leave them in Albuquerque?"

He frowned at her.

"Yeah," his sister said. "It's like that."

She had the gift. She had the dress—and hadn't going to the mall with Magda been a surreal experience? What Julianne wasn't sure she had was the guts to go through with this.

Not to mention any idea what she was going to say.

Fortunately, Kevin's parents chatted virtually nonstop the entire trip, alleviating any worries about having to make small talk. Good thing, since Julianne was half-afraid she'd throw up if she opened her mouth, she was that nervous.

And, if she admitted it, excited.

Pip, of course, sacked out in the car seat the Vaccaros kept in the back of Benny's Pontiac, was completely oblivious to the potentially earth-shattering development in the works.

Eventually the bland highway landscape changed to shaded, winding roads, the occasional glimpse of a mansion in the distance. Then, at last, Benny glanced back and said, as proud as a Jane Austen papa with well-settled daughters, "This is it. Not too shabby, huh?" and a pair of impressive black gates swung open after they were buzzed in. A few minutes' drive up a curved, maple-lined road later revealed a lovely old stone house, elegant but not stuffy, fronted with a dozen stone urns bursting with summer color—petunias, dahlias, marigolds.

And wouldn't Dad love this place? Julianne thought as the car pulled up and a long-haired, long-legged woman about her age in baggy linen pants and a tank top rushed out to embrace Magda and Benny.

The happy, somewhat disheveled bride then zeroed in on Julianne, now out of the car and holding a sleepily blinking Pip. "Ohmigosh..." Mia bent slightly to smile into Pippa's face. "Hi, sweetie," she said, emitting a soft squeal of delight when Pip smiled back. "And you're obviously Julianne." Mia gave her a hug, then held her at arm's length, her ingenuous brown gaze asscessing but not judgmental. "One question—do you love my brother?"

Julianne's vision blurred. "Yes," she said through a thick throat. A bright smile bloomed across the brunette's face.

"Then he's out on the back patio," Mia said. "Just follow the path around the house. Unless…you're not ready?"

"Oh, I'm ready," Julianne said, suddenly aware just how ready she really, truly was.

Slumped in a patio chair that probably cost more than most people spent on their entire living rooms, Kevin flipped his cell phone over and over in his right hand as he glowered at the dozens of worker bees scurrying about erecting tents and setting up tables and whatnot.

So just call the dude, already. Tell him you've changed your mind.

No. Call Julie. Tell her *you've changed your mind.*

Do it, dumbass. Just…call her.

Another five seconds passed before he opened his phone, brought up her number. Weirdly, no less than three people's cells went off at the same time.

The phone rang, once…twice…

"Kevin?" Julie whispered.

He took a deep breath. "Hey, sweetheart. I…" He sat forward, rubbing the space between his eyes, realizing he wasn't sure he could speak. "I miss you guys," he finally got out.

"Yeah," she said, sounding funny. "Me, too."

"So…I've been thinking…that maybe…" He swallowed past the lump in his throat. "Now that I'm here…maybe I was just bein' impatient, you know? Yeah, so this was a great opportunity and all, but who's to say I might not find somethin' just as good in Albuquerque eventually?" When she didn't say anything, he let out a tortured sigh. "Dammit, Julie—I've made so many mistakes in my life, messed up so freaking many times...but I'm thinking this one tops the list. I'm coming back, baby. I need you, in whatever way you'll have me. And being without Pip... It's killin' me, Julie. It's freaking killing me."

"I'm know it is, big guy," she whispered. Except, even more weirdly, it didn't sound like she was on the phone, she sounded—

"Ba-ba-ba-ba-ba-ba," Kevin heard behind him, and he shot out of the chair so fast he nearly knocked it over.

"Okay," he said, his heart going about a thousand miles a minute, "if this'd been two years ago, I'd swear I was hallucinating. Since I'm stone-cold sober..." He extended one trembling hand, swallowing hard. "Holy crap," he whispered, drinking in Julianne's smile, his daughter's drooly grin, and a second later they were all tangled in each other's arms, laughing, crying, hugging, and he breathed in their scents, kissing first Julie, then Pip, then Julie again. "You're really here."

"It would appear so," she said, grinning. Lit up like a damn movie marquee.

He swallowed. "How—"

"We've been staying with your parents since Wednesday. We rode up with them. I adore them both, by the way. But if I start talking in gibberish, you'll understand why."

Kevin laughed. "I know a great cure for that," he said, blinking.

"Oh, yeah? What?"

"This," he said, kissing Julianne long enough to stir a few catcalls and some applause from the worker bees. "All better now?" he said, and she said, "Mmm, getting there. Might take more than one treatment, though," and he said, "Lucky for you, I keep very flexible office hours," and she laughed, and he thought, *Please don't wake up, please don't wake up, please don't—*

"But if you so much as even *think* about giving up that job, there will be hell to pay."

"Julie?" Kevin said over his pounding heart. "What are you saying?"

"That if this is where you need to be—" she took a breath "—then this is where I need to be, too."

"Get out."

"Forget it, I just got here. And take your daughter. She weighs a ton. Then sit. And take notes, because this is a historical moment."

Stunned into silence, Kevin hauled Pip into his arms, every muscle relaxing the moment he had his kid close again. Yeah, it'd only been a cuppla days, but it felt like years. He lowered them both into a glider; the instant it moved, Pip squealed, thrilled.

"Okay," Julianne said, sitting close, her hand on his leg. "This is where I admit I was wrong. Because it turns out…I could fall in love again."

"Really?" Kevin said, hardly daring to breathe.

"Really. Who knew, right?"

"Um…me?"

"And Dad, apparently," she said on a sigh.

Firmly holding Pip around the waist with one arm, Kevin swung the other around Julie's shoulders. "Did you forgive him? About telling me that you can't have kids?"

"I'm working on it," she said, then shifted to look up at him. "Would you have left Pip if he hadn't said anything?"

Kevin hesitated, then said, "I didn't leave her with you because you can't have children. I left her with you because I thought it was best for her."

Julianne snuggled closer. "I would have never, ever stood for that, you know."

"Good thing we're gonna be together, then."

"Yeah. Really good thing." Julie rubbed his thigh for a

moment, then said, "Dad's selling the house. And moving to Virginia to be with Beth."

"You're kidding."

"Nope."

Kevin frowned. "Leaving you all alone."

"Giving me a kick in the pants to start living my own life again, you mean. I'm not here because I have nowhere else to go, Kevin. I'm here because...because I realized *I'd* made a mistake. One I knew I'd regret for the rest of my life if I didn't do something immediately to fix it. Pip needs her daddy." Another pause. "And so do I. Not someday." She smiled up at him. "Right now."

"Oh God, Julie...are you sure? I've still got such a long way to go—"

"Oh, and like I don't? So what the hell, we might as well evolve together, right?"

"Works for me," Kevin said, grinning so hard his cheeks hurt. "Speaking of together...I could really use a date for this shindig tomorrow."

"Then that works out perfectly, since I've got this killer dress that deserves to be drooled over."

"Oh, yeah?"

"Yeah." She leaned over and whispered, "I can't wear anything under it," and Kevin thought he would die on the spot. Then she rested her head on his shoulder. "I'm not looking for another Gil, Kevin," she said gently. Seriously. "Or another daddy figure. Frankly, I think I've had my fill of that," she muttered. "I wasn't *looking* for anything. As you well know." She tilted her face up to his, her eyes brimming with something he'd never seen before. Not for him, anyway. From where he was sitting, it looked a helluva lot like worship, but damned if he was gonna tell her that. "Surprise," she whispered.

He kissed her again. And again, just because. Then she said,

"Now. I've already talked things over with both gallery owners. I can always ship them replacement stock. They'll simply adjust their prices accordingly. I'll have to go back to pack my things and all that, and I suppose I'll need to find a potting studio once we're settled. Oh, and it occurred to me we might as well take the money from the sale of the Seattle place and buy a house here, otherwise I'm just gonna get slammed with capital gains taxes, right? But maybe we should wait to get married until after Dad and Beth do…oh, dear," she said, biting her lip. "Am I moving too fast for you?"

Laughing, Kevin hugged her with one arm, holding Pippa firmly against his chest with the other. "Not at all, honey. Not…at…all."

"Good," she said. "Then…let the worshipping begin."

Kevin laughed loud enough to turn heads from all the way across the yard.

And he held Julie close, worshipping her as much as he dared in public, while their little girl ba-ba-ba'd her approval between them.

* * * * *

Look for LAST WOLF WATCHING
by Rhyannon Byrd—the exciting conclusion
in the BLOODRUNNERS *miniseries*
from Silhouette Nocturne.

Follow Michaela and Brody on their fierce journey to find the truth and face the demons from the past, as they reach the heart of the battle between the Runners and the rogues.

Here is a sneak preview of book three,
LAST WOLF WATCHING.

Michaela squinted, struggling to see through the impenetrable darkness. Everyone looked toward the Elders, but she knew Brody Carter still watched her. Michaela could feel the power of his gaze. Its heat. Its strength. And something that felt strangely like anger, though he had no reason to have any emotion toward her. Strangers from different worlds, brought together beneath the heavy silver moon on a night made for hell itself. That was their only connection.

The second she finished that thought, she knew it was a lie. But she couldn't deal with it now. Not tonight. Not when her whole world balanced on the edge of destruction.

Willing her backbone to keep her upright, Michaela Doucet focused on the towering blaze of a roaring bonfire that rose from the far side of the clearing, its orange flames burning with maniacal zeal against the inky black curtain of the night. Many of the Lycans had already shifted into their preternatural shapes, their fur-covered bodies standing like monstrous shadows at the edges of the forest as they waited with restless expectancy for her brother.

Her nineteen-year-old brother, Max, had been attacked by a rogue werewolf—a Lycan who preyed upon humans for food. Max had been bitten in the attack, which meant he was no longer human, but a breed of creature that existed between the two worlds of man and beast, much like the Bloodrunners themselves.

The Elders parted, and two hulking shapes emerged from the trees. In their wolf forms, the Lycans stood over seven feet tall, their legs bent at an odd angle as they stalked forward. They each held a thick chain that had been wound around their inside wrists, the twin lengths leading back into the shadows. The Lycans had taken no more than a few steps when they jerked on the chains, and her brother appeared.

Bound like an animal.

Biting at her trembling lower lip, she glanced left, then right, surprised to see that others had joined her. Now the Bloodrunners and their family and friends stood as a united force against the Silvercrest pack, which had yet to accept the fact that something sinister was eating away at its foundation—something that would rip down the protective walls that separated their world from the humans'. It occurred to Michaela that loyalties were being announced tonight—a separation made between those who would stand with the Runners in their fight against the rogues and those who blindly supported the pack's refusal to face reality. But all she could focus on was her brother. Max looked so hurt…so terrified.

"Leave him alone," she screamed, her soft-soled, black satin slip-ons struggling for purchase in the damp earth as she rushed toward Max, only to find herself lifted off the ground when a hard, heavily muscled arm clamped around her waist from behind, pulling her clear off her feet. "Damn it, let me down!" she snarled, unable to take her eyes off her brother as the golden-eyed Lycan kicked him.

Mindless with heartache and rage, Michaela clawed at the arm holding her, kicking her heels against whatever part of her captor's legs she could reach. "Stop it," a deep, husky voice grunted in her ear. "You're not helping him by losing it. I give you my word he'll survive the ceremony, but you have to keep it together."

"Nooooo!" she screamed, too hysterical to listen to reason. "You're monsters! All of you! Look what you've done to him! How dare you! *How dare you!"*

The arm tightened with a powerful flex of muscle, cinching her waist. Her breath sucked in on a sharp, wailing gasp.

"Shut up before you get both yourself and your brother killed. I will *not* let that happen. Do you understand me?" her captor growled, shaking her so hard that her teeth clicked together. "Do you understand me, Doucet?"

"Damn it," she cried, stricken as she watched one of the guards grab Max by his hair. Around them Lycans huffed and growled as they watched the spectacle, while others outright howled for the show to begin.

"That's enough!" the voice seethed in her ear. "They'll tear you apart before you even reach him, and I'll be damned if I'm going to stand here and watch you die."

Suddenly, through the haze of fear and agony and outrage in her mind, she finally recognized who'd caught her. *Brody*.

He held her in his arms, her body locked against his powerful form, her back to the burning heat of his chest. A low, keening sound of anguish tore through her, and her head dropped forward as hoarse sobs of pain ripped from her throat. "Let me go. I have to help him. *Please*," she begged brokenly, knowing only that she needed to get to Max. "Let me go, Brody."

He muttered something against her hair, his breath warm against her scalp, and Michaela could have sworn it was a single word.... But she must have heard wrong. She was too upset. Too furious. Too terrified. She must be out of her mind.

Because it sounded as if he'd quietly snarled the word *never*.

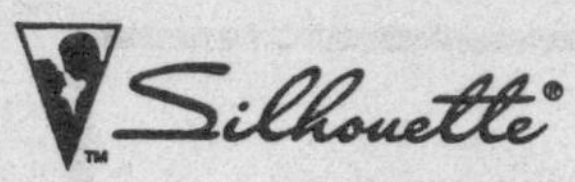

SPECIAL EDITION®

COMING NEXT MONTH

#1897 HER MR. RIGHT?—Karen Rose Smith
The Wilder Family
Social worker Isobel Suarez was proud to work at Walnut River General Hospital, so when Neil Kane showed up from the attorney general's office to investigate insurance fraud, she was up in arms. Until she melted *in* his arms, and things got very tricky....

#1898 THE PRINCE'S ROYAL DILEMMA—Brenda Harlen
Reigning Men
After a freak accident left him in charge of his country and guardian of his brother's three children, Prince Rowan Santiago was overwhelmed. Plus, the law required that the ruler be married by a certain age, and the clock was ticking. There was no shortage of eligible women—but need the prince look any further than royal nanny Lara Brennan?

#1899 THE MILLIONAIRE'S MAKEOVER—Lilian Darcy
Of all of shy garden designer Rowena Madison's demanding clients, English businessman Ben Radford took the cake. But as the work on his exotic garden brought them closer together, Rowena surprised herself—by turning her green thumb to the love blossoming between them!

#1900 THE BABY PLAN—Kate Little
Baby Daze
Levelheaded businesswoman Julia Martinelli didn't believe in romantic nonsense—she wanted a baby, relationship with man optional. After all, look at her mother making a fool of herself with her repairman—and now they were engaged! Ironic, then, when restaurateur Sam Baxter, the repairman's son, stepped in to fix Julia's rigid ideas.

#1901 HER MIRACLE MAN—Karen Sandler
Fate brought Mia to the mountain retreat of self-made millionaire Jack Traynor during a torrential downpour. She had no idea who or where she was; he was still rediscovering himself after being accused of murdering his wife. Never were two souls more in need...of finding each other.

#1902 THEIR SECRET CHILD—Mary J. Forbes
Home to Firewood Island
For years, Addie Trait had dreaded coming face-to-face with the high school sweetheart who'd fled when she'd gotten pregnant, causing her to give the child up for adoption. But now Skip Dalton, with an adorable daughter in tow, was back to coach high school football... and share a very special secret with Addie.

SSECNM0408